COLLECTING CASS

Michael Woodman

Connlaswell Publishing

Copyright

First published in 2024 by Connlaswell Publishing.

Copyright © Michael Woodman 2024

The right of Michael Woodman to be identified as the author of this work has been asserted in accordance with the Copyright, Designs and Patents Act 1988. All the characters in this book, with the exception of those already in the public domain, are fictitious, and any resemblance to actual persons, living or dead, is purely coincidental.

All rights reserved. No part of this publication may be reproduced, stored in a retrieval system or transmitted in any form or by any means without the prior permission in writing of the publisher, nor be otherwise circulated in any form of binding or cover other than that in which it is published without a similar condition, including this condition, being imposed on the subsequent purchaser.

Woodman, Michael. Collecting Cass. Connlaswell Publishing.

ISBN 978-1-7397338-8-9

Men lie. It's a fact. Women lie too, of course. But that's different. Their lies come from the heart. Men's lies...

Her mind drifted, the couple in the photo getting all her attention. Rob, her soon-to-be husband, and Priscilla, his personal assistant. Cass leaned back in her chair, adding a little distance between her and the computer screen. That was the artist in her. Things were not so much what they were as how you looked at them. But whatever angle she looked at this from, she got the same message. It wasn't what they were doing, but the way they were doing it. Had they been naked, entwined in a bed, it would have been better. She'd have been angry then. Anger passed. This was worse. They were sitting side-by-side in a bar, sharing a look. Nothing to it really, not unless you ran it through a who's-fucking-who interpreter.

Ding-a-ling, jackpot.

Eyes and smiles doing all the talking, innocence loaded with contraband, the sweetest of all intimacies, a naughty secret shared. This was a wound so poignant and unexpected it cut deep and would bleed forever. She opened the email headers to figure out who it was from, but she couldn't make sense of them. Too much artist in her and not enough techie. Besides, someone had taken a lot of trouble to deliver this unexpected news bulletin anonymously. Her phone rang and she spun her head looking for it, but it was nowhere on the desk. The ringing was muted and distant. She swiveled her chair and peered out through the French doors of the summerhouse and into the sunlit garden beyond.

It was on the table on the terrace, perched next to the iced tea she'd been drinking earlier.

Let it ring.

It would be Rob telling her he was on his way home. Yes, let it ring. This was not the moment for idle chitchat with him.

Men's lies, she thought—getting back on track, her eyes narrowing in on the photo—ugly as it sounded, came from their dicks. And here was the proof, an anonymous email from a "Good Samaritan" according to the sender field.

This was how the bad thing started, a brutal revelation of an infidelity. A hollow silence followed, interrupted by the phone again. It rang and rang, ringing unattended like it always did in a black and white noir movie, a creepy one, where a lone heroine got threatened by a dangerous male brute. But you can forget all that. Cass belonged in the twenty-first century, not a creaky old movie, and she could take care of herself.

Fear and excitement churned in his belly, switching him on and off like a bulb on the blink. He slipped his hand into the breast pocket of his overalls and fiddled with the ski mask, running its coarse wool through his trembling fingers. He didn't pull it out. Not yet. Too soon. The touch and feel of it was all he wanted, a comfort blanket. He started the van, turned the corner at the end of the road and cruised along the street.

Her street.

No problem with that, nothing suspicious. There was no one in sight, and even if someone had peered out from one of the luxury homes that bordered it, all they'd have seen was a gardener on his way to a customer's house. In an upscale neighborhood like this, gardeners were the invisible men, so ubiquitous they didn't even register on the retinas of passers-by. He hunched over the wheel as he passed her house, scanning the tree-lined walls of the properties in the immediate vicinity and giving their electric gates special attention. They all had cameras focused tight on the entrance where they'd get a clear shot of any vehicles waiting to enter and any person standing there. They'd catch anyone walking by too, but not passing traffic in the roadway, at least nothing more than a glimpse of wheels and paneling. No new cameras anywhere. Everything was just as it had been the last time he'd checked, grand houses on lots of an acre or more, hidden behind walls and swathes of greenery, plenty of work for plenty of gardeners. He pulled in to the curb and parked, the exact location predetermined, a blind spot between two houses. He'd even checked the tech data on the camera models and run simulations.

Don't puke!

Not an idle admonition that. His guts were twisting and it had happened before at this very spot.

Why is real so different?

His rehearsals were flawless. But the gap between those imagined triumphs and his lived disasters was an ever-growing chasm. In his head, he had balls of steel. Too bad they weren't hanging between his legs. He closed his eyes, drew a deep breath, then let it out with a sigh as his eyes popped open.

Do it.

Afraid he'd lose the moment and see his pinch of courage washed away by fear once again, he grabbed his bag from the passenger seat and stepped out of the van, his movements jerky and robotic.

See it. Believe it. She's yours. Take her.

He checked his watch.

Forty-five minutes max.

Her man would be home by then. He never came sooner and often later, always with a plausible excuse, a zoom session with the big shots in New York was a favorite while *shagging my PA in a hotel near the office* never made the cut.

That was the window, and Sharpe had forty-five minutes to make it real. He felt in his pocket again—yes, the mask was still there—and stepped into the alley, the footpath that wound between her property and her neighbor's. It was walled on both sides and led to a wooded area frequented by dog walkers. But there were none there now. There was no one on the path or in the street. People in this affluent neighborhood had their cycles, their rote behaviors, and this was too early for Fido's evening walk and too late for his afternoon outing. Sharpe hurried along it, his boots scuffing ground hardened by a thousand footsteps, the walls on either side looming higher and the trees above him knotting their branches tighter with every pace. His heart hammered. This was only a footpath, not a tunnel, not a trap closing in on him. It just felt like that. He stumbled against the wall, supporting himself with one hand against it and half hoping a dog walker would appear at the end of the alley. He'd have to abandon then. No choice. But no such savior appeared. More breaths, not long and easy like in the van, but sharp and raspy like a dead man grabbing the last of his life. He pushed himself off the wall and made the remaining few steps at a trot, stopping at a heavy wooden door set in the wall. Ancient and neglected, it looked like something from a bygone era, something forgotten, with weeds growing thick at its base and counting the years since it had last swung open. He looked both ways.

Nobody.

His ears strained, secretly hoping for any untoward sound, anything to flash a red light and send him scuttling back to the van. But all he could hear was the rustling of trees, bird songs and the hum of bees, the soundtrack of a perfect summer day in the English countryside. He pulled the mask from his pocket and put it on, then reached into his bag and pulled out a prybar. The scrape of its metal against the wood and rusty lock sent a shiver through him. He was running out of time, but he couldn't rush this crucial step.

Will she come easy? Will it all work?

With one final push, the lock gave way and the door creaked open. He peeked through the crack into darkness with the wall, the trees and bushes turning sunlight into twilight. No matter. He smiled under the mask. He was doing it at last. Where was his fear, his cursed sidekick? Flattened by reality. He was doing it for real, fear flushed into ether, courage burning furnace hot. He stepped through the gate into the darkness.

A phone....

He froze.

It was ringing somewhere. He crept forward and with gloved fingertips edged aside branches of summer green leaves. There it was on that table outside the summerhouse.

So where's Cass?

The phone rang and rang.

3

Why answer it? What was the point?

Far better to wait until Rob got home, then confront him with the evidence. If she picked up that phone, she'd blow it. No way could she hold this in. It was already ripping a hole in her middle. No way could she cloak it in a loving tone and coo welcome-home-darling words of love. It would spill out of her mouth the moment she heard his voice. Spill as in tsunami. Then he wouldn't come home. He'd waffle an excuse, hang up, then spend the night with Priscilla or with his buddy Monty, smoking pot and reminiscing about how wonderful life had been back in their student days.

So she ignored it.

But it rang again.

How many times is that?

Two, three? That's not like Rob. No one got his attention for that long, not even her. She stood up, still hoping it would stop, and shuffled barefoot out through the French doors and onto the terrace. She dragged a chair out from under the table, its filigreed metal legs scraping and skipping on the uneven stone tiles.

"Is he home yet?" A posh British voice demanded. A female one. No *Hi*. No *how's your day going*? None of that polite stuff, and pointedly nothing remotely friendly. This was a tough moment. Her jaw snapped shut, teeth skidding back-and-forth.

How is this going to go?

A string of expletives? Threats? This was the woman in the photo, and Cass so wanted to go there.

"Hello, Priscilla," she said, opting for a needle instead of a sword. Priscilla hated her name. It reeked of what she was, the child of bottom-feeding aristocrats so cash poor they'd had to eat dog food to pay her school bills. So everyone, including Rob, called her Pix or Pixie. Cute name, charming even. Everything she was not. "What's up? No he isn't." Cass checked the time. "Still on his way, I guess."

"He's not answering his phone."

"So, maybe he's stuck in a tunnel or—"

"There was a detective here with a uniformed cop. Like they have when they arrest someone. Right here in the bloody office."

"What did they want?"

"Rob. They wanted to speak to him."

"What kind of detective?"

"What does it matter?"

"I mean... was something stolen? Someone murdered?"

"It's that financial task force thingy, serious crime something. Our New York office got served with papers the other day. Did he tell you about that?"

The answer was no, but that was the last thing that would come out of her mouth.

"It's probably some routine compliance thing."

"In *this* country, cops don't show up at offices for... Oh, forget it. If they do show up before Rob gets home, you know nothing. Do you understand?"

"You don't need to tell me that. Know what about what?"

"Just act dumb." She hung up.

Cass dropped the phone on the table—now she wished she'd gone for the sword—and stared out through the trees towards the house.

The garden was a picture with late afternoon sunlight filtering through leaves, casting dappled shadows on the lawn. A beautiful summer's evening was about to begin. But not for Cass. She picked up the chamomile tea she'd left by the phone earlier and took a sip. If ever there was a moment calling for a calming brew, this was it, although Jim Beam would have been her first choice.

Detective?

Logical explanations skimmed through her head, but none of them stuck. Rob had mentioned compliance issues a few times lately. But what did that mean exactly? Compliance? Wasn't that lawyer-speak for staying out of jail? Crypto was cowboy country with fuzzy laws, few sheriffs, and an endless digital landscape to hide in. But the dreary world of stocks and shares with its stack of paperwork was catching up fast. New York, legal papers, the Feds? Rob hadn't mentioned any of it. Not a good sign. She stood up. The garden was buzzing with life—bees, birds, the whole package, a sweet spot moment in the English summer. As she went back into the summerhouse, she heard something in the bushes by the wall.

A fox?

They were absurdly nonchalant in this area with no fear of humans, wandering in and out of gardens at will.

No, not a fox.

That was a knock. Someone in the alley with a dog heading for the woods, throwing a stick most likely. She passed through the open French doors and headed for the computer.

That photo.

Was she reading too much into it?

It was something. But it was nothing too. If they'd been in a clinch, she could have confronted Priscilla. She could have—

The phone again...

Cass let it ring. She was done with it, in no mood for conversation, the day's events rattling in her head far too loud.

The phone stopped and started again.

She got to her feet, ground down by it. Staring at the photo was pointless. It was never going to make sense. Rob and Cass were the perfect couple, weren't they? Everyone said so. The question lingered unanswered. There had to be a reason their wedding had been postponed twice. Was this it? She headed back out onto the terrace, her bare feet brushing against the cool wooden floor. The phone stopped ringing as she picked it up.

She checked the caller. Rob.

She turned and—

"Aagh..."

A masked man...

The shock left her breathless, frozen. He grabbed her, one hand looping behind her head and grabbing her hair, the other thrusting a stinking cloth against her face. She lashed out with a kick, her shin arcing up between his legs and catching him in the groin. Not a good shot. She was standing too close, no leverage. But it worked. He grunted and stumbled back half a step, releasing her for a split second. She pushed him aside and ran into the summerhouse, turned and threw her body weight against the door. But his weight was on the other side of it and he was heavier. Still, it was working until he jammed the door with his foot.

Weapon.

The summerhouse had a kitchenette with a fridge, a sink and enough cutlery to handle an occasional barbecue on the terrace.

Knives.

There were sharp ones in a wooden block by the sink.

If she could...

She ran to the kitchen, the door exploding open behind her. Three steps into it, he tackled her and she hit the floor, its hard wood knocking the wind out of her with a pained cry. She kicked and wriggled free, then crawled up on all fours. But he was on her again as she stood up, and they tumbled headlong with him on top, her elbows cracking the floor. She screamed, momentarily paralyzed, pain shooting up her arms to her neck. He grabbed her legs, pinning them with his bodyweight. She was face down, clawing at the floor, but it did no good. He was crawling up her, bit by bit. She slammed her bruised elbow back—once, twice. He twisted away to avoid the blows and—

My phone.

He'd knocked it out of her hands. It was lying there, right under the desk.

If I could—

That stinking rag was on her face again, its acrid stench making her gag. All it would take was two deep breaths and she'd keel over. She snapped her head to the side, her lips finding leather. A gloved hand. She bit hard. He howled and jerked back, and free of his weight, she squirmed away from him. He had one hand on the floor supporting himself, the other held up by his face, nursing a bloodied finger.

"Siri... Call Rob."

The man froze, brown eyes in the slit of his mask lit with panic.

Yes, Cass heard it too... the joyous and unmistakable sound of Rob's phone ringing. He went for her again, rag first. She grabbed his face, scratching his eyes. She had to buy time, another whiff of that stuff and she'd be out of it. He knocked her arms away. But her fingers caught in the eyeholes in the mask and it slewed to the side revealing his face. Not all of it. But enough.

I know him.

The ringing stopped. "I'm on my way, darling." The purr of Rob's car in the background—his beloved Bentley—gave her a jolt of hope and a spike of adrenaline. If he stormed through that door and saved her, she'd forgive him anything. "A man..." It was all she got out—screeching it— before the man grabbed her throat and shut her mouth with his rag. "Cass... Is everything okay?" She clawed at his eyes again. And he released her throat, grabbing her arm and pinning it to the floor with his knee. But that took seconds and she didn't waste one of them. "I've seen this bastard..." The man clamped the cloth on her mouth. She grabbed his wrist and swept it aside momentarily. "At the office." But those few seconds were all she got. He looped one arm behind her neck and held the cloth to her mouth, all his weight on top of her. She thrashed, her limbs flailing. But that knockout dose of chemical stink was too strong. Its fumes burned her nostrils and nausea gripped her as she spiraled down, her muscles weakening, her struggles fading.

No escape now.

Then she was gone.

4

Sharpe stood over her, head spinning.

She was on the floor, unconscious, the phone inches from her hand. It had all gone so wrong. The French doors were wide open behind him.

Freedom called.

Run for it.

It wasn't too late. He could abort.

What other choice did he have?

But he didn't move. He couldn't. Feet, arms, legs, nothing worked. Data overload. Too much happening too fast, and none of it in the plan.

It was a bust. That phone call.

I've seen this bastard at the office.

The thunderbolt moment. She'd remembered his face after so much time. How was that possible? Did she remember his name too?

Ted Sharpe.

Were those the next words out of her mouth? His name, his identity, broadcast to her boyfriend, the game over before it had begun.

If he hadn't stuffed that rag in her mouth, it might have been. But what now? That phone call. Was it game over?

No... if she remembers my name, I have to take her, or else—

"Cass, Cass..."

He spun around. The call was still connected and Rob Washington was screaming his lungs out. He'd race like hell to get home.

How long would it take him?

No answers anywhere, and the questions got worse.

What if he called the police? They'd be here in minutes.

"You bastard," Washington roared, giving up on Cass and filling in the blanks. "If you hurt her, I'll beat the shit out of you. I'll—" Sharpe stood motionless, the threats hitting him like punches in the gut, anger sweeping aside his run-for-it instinct and driving him back to the phone. He snatched it up. No plan. Pure reflex. White heat driving him, bursting his heart.

"You're nothing," he screamed, cutting short Washington's rant. "She's mine now. You call the police I'll kill her." He flung the phone with a sweep of his arm and it thudded against the wall with a tinkle of glass.

For a moment, that was it. He stood motionless, stunned.

I'll kill her?

He'd said that. He'd actually said it.

Cass groaned and rolled on her side, coughing like she might throw up. Sharpe slipped off his backpack and pulled a syringe from its front pocket. She jerked up suddenly and tried to stand up, wobbling on all fours. He stepped astride her, pinning her sides with his legs, then held her neck with one hand and poked the syringe into her shoulder. Back on plan at last. He'd researched sedative options and picked Valium because he could shoot it into the muscle. It might not work as well as IV. But if he'd had to find a vein, he would have needed the cloth again to quieten her, and after that phone call, there was no time for that. He held her a moment to let the shot circulate, then stepped back. In seconds, her body eased down to the floor and he hoisted her up over his shoulder. She was heavy and awkward. He'd practiced carrying a sack stuffed with two 25 kg bags of potatoes he'd bought from a neighboring farm. That was more or less her weight. 54 kilos, or 120 pounds to her, being an American. She'd posted her weight in a yoga forum. But at 5'8" she was more unwieldy than a sack of potatoes, and that made his progress slow as he swiveled out through the French doors and staggered across the lawn towards the trees. He laid her down in the long grass by the old door in the wall. He was panting and needed a moment to get his breath, but he had no—

"Daisy... come away." An old woman's voice, screechy and close.

In the alley, by the door.

Sharpe froze, locking his chest tight to quieten its heaving. He'd left the door open. Too much grass and weeds growing there had made it difficult to close. It wasn't open much. Just a foot, maybe less. He slid his back against the wall, getting closer to the open crack between the door and the wall. If the dog came through that gap, the old woman would follow. She'd see Cass. She'd see him—

Damn!

He still had the ski mask on. He'd nearly stepped out into the road with it on. In the middle of summer! But forgetting it had been a stroke of luck. If the woman saw him now, at least—

"Daisy... I won't tell you again."

Her dog was right there, feet away, his head poked through the gap. A terrier type, tiny, with a salt-and-pepper face and one good eye staring up at Sharpe. Just one eye. The other was a puckered scar, grayed with age, a memento perhaps of an encounter with an alley cat that didn't go his way. The old lady was sure to see him now.

But no.

There was a flash of black as her arm reached into the crack and her dog was gone. He breathed easy, slid up to the door and peeked out towards the woods. The woman was on her way, the dog bundled under one arm still peering at him from over her shoulder.

Sharpe pulled off the ski mask, spun out into the alley and strode back to the van. He pulled out a roll of black plastic sheeting, 6 mm heavy duty stuff. It was advertised as multiuse, although its manufacturers surely didn't have abduction in mind. He'd precut it to length. So all he had to do was lay it out next to Cass, then roll her over onto it. It took him less than a minute to have her bundled up and hoisted up on his shoulder. In three minutes, he was in the driver's seat, starting the engine.

No cops in sight.

If her man had put in the call, they'd be here by now. His gamble had paid off. Washington would think twice after that threat.

He turned the corner at the end of the road.

No sign of Washington's precious Bentley careening through the leafy lanes to save her. That was all good. But it didn't stop his body stiffening over the wheel. It wasn't done yet, and now that rush of adrenaline was wearing off, fear was sneaking back into him, tightening his muscles and shortening his breath. He drove his planned route, handcrafted to avoid the Bentley. A nondescript black gardener's van was hardly a red flag waving abduction. But why take the risk? He drove out of Cobham, passing its grand estates with their sculpted hedges and manicured lawns. It wasn't until he'd picked up the B2039, a two-lane blacktop, and was driving its dips and curves through lush green woods, that his iron stiff body softened and slumped against the backrest. He looked over his shoulder to check on Cass. He hadn't bound her. Too risky. It would have taken too long. Besides, that Valium shot was enough to knock out a horse.

Should I tie her, make sure?

He checked his watch. He had one hour and forty minutes to drive, and for a moment he was second-guessing his decision to avoid the motorways and major roads. But he put those doubts behind him when he reached sprawling fields of barley and wheat and saw flashes of rolling chalk hills in the distance. His route avoided villages and towns. But in southeast England, that wasn't entirely possible, and a few moments gave him pause. He hurried those stretches as best he could, mindful of the radar traps in many of them. So it wasn't until he glimpsed a thatched-roof cottage tucked away down a tree-lined lane that it hit him.

I've done it.

He took a deep breath—it felt like the first one he'd ever had in his life—and let it go with a smile. He stopped by a wooden farm gate next to a rusty Private Property sign. In the fading light, both were almost invisible, hidden in the hedgerow. He got out of the van, unlocked the chain securing it to a wonky post and dragged open its creaking timbers. Driving through, he didn't go back to lock it. No point. It wasn't meant to keep people out. It was cosmetic, letting passers by—in the unlikely event that there were any—know that beyond the gate lay nothing special, another ordinary farm like the last one you passed.

Nothing to see here. Move along, please.

A few hundred yards into the woods, he came to the property's actual gate, solid metal, set in a brick wall mounted with infrared CCTV cameras. He clicked a remote, and as it rumbled open, he glanced back at Cass.

"You're home, Cass. We finally made it after all these years."

The gravel driveway beyond the wall led to a timber-framed farmhouse hung with wall tiles. Dating back to the sixteenth century, it looked every year of its age. He drove across its stony courtyard and parked the van in a converted granary that served as a multicar garage. Built at the same time as the house, it bore all the same scars of old age, its tiles a patchwork of reds and grays strewn with cracks. He carried Cass to the house, through the hallway and down the stairs to the basement. It was everything you'd expect, dimly lit, boxes and barrels, a single door leading off of it, and a wine rack taking up an entire wall. With Cass still perched on his shoulder, he pulled a wine bottle from the rack—a carefully chosen one—and placed it on top of a barrel. The rack slid to the side, revealing a steel door with a glass screen on it. He put his palm against the screen and the door popped open. Lights came on as he entered a hallway in stark contrast to the house above. It was modern, minimalist and tasteful. He carried her through the living room and into a bedroom where he laid her on a king-sized bed dwarfed by the size of the room.

He hurried out. It had been two hours since he'd given her that shot. The last thing he wanted was another disaster like their fight in the summerhouse, like that damn phone call. He closed the steel door, but left the wine rack where it was and went through the door next to it into his control room. The hum that greeted him was a comfort. It always was. The sound came from two racks of servers and routers going about their business, and from the instant he'd first heard that sound as a child, he'd known what it was. Information, power, magic. His lullaby. He sat at a desk and fired up a laptop, waiting as images flooded the CCTV screens on the wall opposite. Every room in her basement apartment was covered. Almost. He didn't want cameras in every room. That wouldn't be right. Cass deserved some privacy. So her bathroom and dressing room were exempt. He adjusted the camera feeds. No point in looking at empty rooms. There was only one thing he wanted to see.

Cass.

And there she was with eight cameras giving him every conceivable angle and focus. Her face. He zoomed in closer and closer still. She flicked her hand, loosely touching her nose, a reflex. Her eyes were still closed, but she'd be waking up about now. No rush. She wasn't going anywhere. Satisfied that all was well, he dimmed the screens. There'd be plenty of time to sit and stare, and Cyclops, his surveillance server, required his attention. Cyclops was the internet node that ran his eavesdropping and hacking programs. Not spying on Cass now, but her supposed, soon-to-be husband. No CCTV available, but that didn't matter. Sharpe had infected Washington's phone with spyware, a neat trick, and not much of a challenge for a onetime analyst at GCHQ, Britain's NSA. He scrolled through the logs, all the calls Washington had made and received since the last check.

The lad's been busy...

But then he stopped when the phone's geolocation tab caught his eye. That was where Washington was located right now—Kew, Surrey—a London borough famous for its botanical gardens, although Washington was certainly not enjoying its exotic flora. The location beacon was moving. So he hadn't yet arrived. But Sharpe knew where he was going, and he was almost there. He was visiting his old mate, Monty, a college friend who'd been parachuted out of Durham University after narrowly escaping a custodial sentence for dealing cocaine. So hours after his wife was abducted, he wasn't at home with a battalion of cops in forensic suits, but hanging out with his bestie.

Sharpe smiled.

Only one explanation...

He double-checked the logs again. No calls to the police. His threat—*I'll kill her*—had worked. He fingered the keyboard excitedly, connected to Washington's phone, and leaned back in his chair, adjusting his comfort like a theatergoer looking forward to a great show.

"So he took her? Like... kidnapped?" That was Monty's voice. Washington had arrived and blurted out the news as he walked through the door. There was a pause with no response from Washington. Rustling sounds, the two of them getting settled. Sharpe turned on the visual feed, but it didn't help much. All he could see was the trendy chandelier in Monty's living room, a cluster of brightly lit glass spheres held in place by black rods. He'd often monitored their conversations here. So he could picture the rest. The phone would be on the Moroccan style hexagonal table in the center of the room with Washington and Monty lounging on the comfy sofas surrounding it. No worries. Sharpe didn't need video to follow events. He could guess Washington's silent response. He'd be nodding or shrugging. He was a great communicator with his body, especially when he had nothing to say. "What about the police?"

"He threatened to kill her if I called them."

It worked.

Sharpe's smile burst its seams and he laughed, its aftermath a girly giggle in his throat.

"You didn't call the cops?" Once again, no audible reply, just a stream of blue smoke clouding the lights in the chandelier. "They always say that. He was freaked out by that phone call. Calling you on Siri, boy, that was smart. The guy had to be shocked. He couldn't have planned for it. So what could he do? Threaten you and hope is all."

"I don't know if it's a bluff. What if I bring in the cops? Then four months down the road they find her chopped up in a suitcase in a canal." Another stream of smoke. Washington was really hitting the weed. "Maybe you could live with that, but I couldn't."

"So what's the plan? You wait until they ask for cash, then—"

"Pay, of course."

"Did she see his face?"

"Someone from the office, she said. But that makes no sense. Who'd do that? They'd never get away with it."

"You've got to call the cops. If he saw her face..."

Monty's sentence faded into an ominous silence.

"What are you saying? He'll kill her anyway?"

Now it was Monty's turn to duck a question, no comfortable answer to that one. Finally, he said, "I'm just saying I'd call the cops."

Sharpe wasn't smiling anymore. There was every chance Monty might persuade him to make that call. They'd been friends for years, friends and more, confidants, routinely sharing secrets.

"Today has been unreal, a Technicolor horror show. I—"

"What else happened?"

"A detective came by the office asking for me."

"Why?"

"Some investigation that started in the US. Lord knows what those guys have been up to. Ever since the feds nailed Bankman-Fried—"

"Who?"

"That FTX crypto exchange guy. Ever since then, they've had a hard-on for the whole sector. And you know how it is if the FBI cracks a whip, our guys jump like crickets."

"So, what are you telling me? You didn't call the cops because the guy threatened Cass, or because they're investigating you?"

"Hey… that's not what I said. You're reading way too much into this. They're not investigating me. It's the New York office. I'm just telling you about my shitty day." Sharpe caught a flash of Washington's face as he stood up and slipped into the camera's frame momentarily. "Want another beer?" A long beat of silence followed as he fetched more cold ones from the fridge. Sharpe waited, following the muted sound of a TV in the background. It was barely audible. Football. Man City versus Liverpool. A great match. But no takers in this house. Not on a day like this. Washington's arm reached across the table with a can of beer in it. "Is it okay if I stay here tonight? I can't face being in that house without her."

"What if the kidnapper calls?"

"It gets forwarded to me." The screen went blank as Washington's big hand picked up his phone.

Sharpe grunted. Good luck with that. There'd be no calls from this kidnapper.

He logged out of the conversation. He'd already had the best of it and by leaving the server on record, he could pick up the rest of it later. He tuned back in to the CCTV monitors, leaping to his feet when the image of Cass came through. She'd moved. She was still on the bed and still unconscious, but…

He couldn't leave her like that.

She must have stood up and fallen back on the bed, or else she'd writhed around and….

He marched out of the control room and hurried through the apartment to her bedroom without closing the door behind him. Even if she woke up, she'd be manageable, he thought. No way would she make a run for it in that state. He stood by the bed looking down at her. The way she was lying was all wrong. She'd moved to the middle of the bed with her head and shoulders facing one way and her hips squirmed the other. She was wearing a summery dress, shapely but not tight. Thin cotton. Not a fancy designer item. Something to feel comfortable in at home on a warm day, a dress that would double up as a nightgown, its top half split in the front to her breasts and closed with a cotton tie in a bow. It was loose around her waist and had ended up twisted around her hips exposing her white panties. He couldn't see all of them, but enough to bring him to a shuddering halt, frozen with indecision. He couldn't leave her like that. When she woke up, she'd think he'd done something to her, touched her.

Or worse.

His eyes traced the contours on the inside of her thighs, the way they swept up to...

He took a step back, a spinning wheel in his head making him dizzy, his eyes still nailed to that spot.

Nailed to it.

The shape of it, the way it...

He closed his mouth and swallowed, shuffling closer, his heart a drumbeat, his breath a staccato wheeze. He bent over her and reached down, his hands moving slowly like he was grabbing a snake. They drifted either side of her hips and he took hold of the dress between his thumbs and index fingers, barely brushing her skin. Then he tugged, his unemployed fingers fanning outward so as not to touch her. Gently pulling, he slid the dress down, covering the mound, then stepped back.

One, two.

Quick steps.

That was better. But it still wasn't right. The ties closing the top of her dress had broken in the struggle and her breasts were showing, one of them anyway. Not completely. But enough to see her nipple, enough to make her think he'd groped her. He couldn't have that. Inching forward, he bent over her. This was going to be tricky. He lifted one side of the dress and peeked under it. No bra. So much for his *adjust the bra* plan. If he tried to sort it out, he'd end up groping her. He wrung his hands to get the shakes out of them. No, that wouldn't be right. He was not a groper, a molester, a scumbag. He went to the closet and took out a sheet from the linen shelf at the top. Spotless and ironed starchy crisp, he billowed it out over her and let it settle like a parachute in a faint breeze. That was better. Now she wouldn't think he'd done anything dirty. She could check herself out if she doubted it. Just a few bruises—on her arms mostly—and she'd know where they'd come from. He'd apologize for them, for being so rough with her. None of that was supposed to happen.

"I'll make it up to you," he said.

He stood looking down at her after that, still something troubling him. Still not perfect. He tucked the sheet in around her and adjusted her head on the pillow, bolder now her female parts were out of sight. He fanned her blond hair out on either side, its silky threads running through his fingers.

Couldn't be more perfect.

He took a snapshot, not with his camera. That was in the control room. Besides, he didn't need to. The CCTV was running. He had it all on video. His shot was the indelible kind, burned into his mind's eye, an image that could never be erased. He stashed it in his catalog, the one entitled *Dreams Fulfilled,* and headed for the door.

5

Her eyelids fluttered, her mind foggy and disoriented.

Cass slid her hands up her body and buried her face in its spread fingers. Her head throbbed, every heartbeat a pulse of pain hammering into her eyeballs. She sucked a deep breath in through the mouth to still the raging storm inside her. But the lingering stench of chemicals clung to her nostrils like glue. She struggled up onto her elbows, the urge to vomit racking her guts, and scanned the room. Dark, just colored LEDs, with a dim glow of a new day a faint promise from windows high on the wall. She rolled her body, sliding her feet down to the floor and sitting on the edge of the bed. Yes, it was a bed. She couldn't think straight or see much of anything, but she'd gotten that far. Her body rocked, looking for balance. Too much movement, too quickly. Her queasy belly squirted acid into her throat and she jerked up onto her feet and stumbled towards the door by the bed and the soft light beyond it.

She pushed it open.

A bathroom.

She fell against the vanity, arched over the sink and heaved.

Once, twice.

She ran the tap and splashed water on her face, then cupped handfuls of it, washing her mouth out and pumping it in and out of her nose. Cleaned up, she felt better. She felt terrible, but that was a quantum improvement from where she'd been at. She opened the tap to max, washing away the stench of it all and steadying herself against the vanity with her palms resting on its cool top. Beat by beat, her raging heart calmed, and she hit the switch next to the nightlight, turning on a warm background glow. Instinctively, she splashed more water around the sink, grateful for the jars of herbs scattered on the marble-topped double vanity.

Herbs... aromatherapy?

That stopped her dead, her eyes shifting gears, looking around her as if for the first time. Sleek stoneware vessel sinks, brass faucets, an iron soaking tub with claw feet, a sauna, a walkaround shower and a whirlpool bath with shiny fittings.

Where the hell am I?

She tried to make sense of it... at home in Cobham, the summerhouse, the photo, the phone call, the news about the detective, the masked man. House invasion had been her first thought. But he'd kidnapped her. This was the reality, an abduction.

Who kidnaps a woman from her own home in broad daylight?

Money?

It had to be money. But then again...

She gave the bathroom another once over.

Shouldn't she be locked in a closet, whimpering in darkness amid brooms and brushes? Or in a grimy basement, dank and dark, with rats shuffling in the corner. But instead, she had this, a show house bathroom beamed in directly from *Architectural Digest*. It was so obviously the work of an interior designer it might have had her signature on the wall. With everything that had happened, noticing this might seem odd. But Cass was a graduate of the Royal College of Art, whose alumni included world-famous artists, designers, and even an Oscar-winning director. With that on her resume, this bathroom was unlikely to escape her attention. No, she wasn't giving out prizes or rating the work from one to ten. But she couldn't get the strangeness of it out of her head, the *Alice in Wonderland* quality of the rabbit hole she'd been dragged into.

If not money, then...

Did he...?

Instinctively, she ran her hands over her body.

No. She'd feel it. Wouldn't she?

She went back to the summerhouse, running through the snapshots in her head, finally getting to—

Rob!

She'd called him.

He knows.

There'd be cops looking for her already, checking CCTV, interviewing neighbors. She groaned with relief. Whatever crazy nightmare she'd stumbled into, it wasn't going to last. Rob might be a cheating bastard. But underneath the hip, millennial millionaire status image he cultivated, he was old school, a chip off his dad's blue-collar block. No way would he let another man grab his woman and make off with her like some kind of fucking trophy. She dried her face and hands on a soft white towel, the movement triggering an avalanche of aches and pains.

Is there any part that doesn't hurt?

Her eyes drifted back to the iron tub. An hour's rest in piping hot water would be bliss, but she had other priorities, and top of the list was getting the lay of the land and figuring out what in hell's name was going on. She went into the bedroom and turned on the light.

A dimmer switch.

She set it on low and sat on the edge of the bed, her arms thrust like pillars at her sides, holding her steady as she ruminated on what she knew and speculated about what she didn't. The masked man, the chloroform—or whatever it was—the violence and abduction. But then, no closet, no dingy basement, no rats, but luxury. She looked down at her hands resting on silky soft sheets, Egyptian cotton from the feel of them. Dingy, it certainly wasn't. But judging by the diffused natural light filtering in through frosted glass at the top of one wall, it had to be a basement. There were no other windows. So no way of knowing where it might be located. A wooden dresser was decorated with a stone sculpture, fresh flowers in a ceramic vase and a vintage clock. Next to the dresser was a food cart, a catering trolley the Brits called it, a round one with a silver tray on top. She crossed the room and checked out its contents—finger-cut, crust-free sandwiches arranged on bone china plates. On the middle shelf was a thermal coffeepot. She flipped the lid.

Oh, lordy....

She'd only opened it for a second, but that Blue Mountain spiciness was unmistakable. Chocolatey, nutty. She poured a cup. Yes, it might be poisoned or drugged, but since whoever had abducted her could have killed her by now, there was no point in worrying about such things. She sipped the coffee and breathed its aroma deep inside her. It felt like a scouring pad cleaning her from the inside out. The sandwiches were made just the way she liked them with white and whole-wheat bread. She peeled off the wrap tucked around the plate and checked their contents—smoked salmon, Alaskan wild-caught judging by the color, and French cheeses with sliced cucumbers, the crunchy Japanese kind, her favorite.

She put the coffee down, eyes scanning the rest of the room, that pre-puke, queasy feeling returning, and it wasn't the smell of the food or the hot coffee troubling her belly. It was the matchless perfection of all this as if some magical AI had stuck a wire into her brain and hatched out her dream bedroom to match her dream bathroom.

Through the bedroom's open doorway, she could see a living room and a hallway beyond it. But they could wait. The bedroom still had secrets. That door opposite, for example—she hadn't checked it yet—a quilted door next to the bathroom. She strode across the room, the caffeine sharpening her step.

It was a walk-in closet. She'd expected as much. But she hadn't expected a dressing room like this. Cabinets with hanging racks and custom storage areas, full-length mirrors front and back, a makeup vanity with recessed lighting, a seating area with an ottoman, display cases stuffed with handbags, sunglasses, and other collectibles she whizzed by too fast to catch. Cass stood at the center of it all and turned and turned, her eyes twirling in their sockets.

It was chock-full.

There was not an empty space anywhere. The racks, the drawers and cubbyholes, all of them were stacked. She checked the clothes, already afraid, feeling it before knowing it. Yes, everything was her size, every label was her first choice, and not just the names she'd pulled out her plastic for, but every designer whose webpage she'd ever drooled over. It was her closet, her dream closet. She jumped back, her hands covering her face. No more queasy, not even frightened. Try terrified. Someone had emptied her mind into this closet.

No, not my mind, my browser, my phone, my laptop.

That little shit, that toad-faced man in a ski mask, had scraped every wish list she'd ever written and unzipped a bottomless pocketbook to pay for it.

Who was he?

However hard she beat back through her memories, it wouldn't come to her. It didn't matter anyway.

Remembering was just a point of pride at this point and rage soon hustled it away.

"Yes, yes, yes... you... ahhh."

Rob's voice...

Cass burst out of the dressing room.

He had to be here already, his voice so loud that—

Her eyes went up to the wall TV.

A video recording... he's taped us fucking.

He must have bugged the house and—

"Aargh..."

The screen lit up. An unfamiliar room.

No, not our house. She could tell by the lamp fixtures, the corner of the headboard and the decorations. He'd bugged Rob's phone, and it had to be on a nightstand somewhere. Her body sank with the sudden realization of what she was witnessing.

That's not our bedroom.

"You juicy bastard"—Pix, unmistakably Pix—"you nearly drowned me." She reared up on the edge of the viewport, licking her lips, naked, hair askew.

The TV died and silence followed. Cass buried her face in her hands, girding herself, stiffening up on the inside as best she could. This was torture. Intentional torture. Toadface was doubling down on the photo he'd sent. That had been his opening round, light sparring, softening her up for a gut punch way below the belt. She'd gone from hope—Rob's here, my savior—to a black pit of despair inside a dozen heartbeats. Fearing the worst after seeing a photo was hurtful enough. Witnessing it so graphically, Pix's face rearing up in triumph over her man, her mouth still wet with his lust, was unbearable. But bear it, she must. She had to stop those tears. There were cameras looking at her, had to be.

Suck it up.

She'd be damned before giving him the pleasure of her pain.

The TV lit up again, and there was Toadface sitting in front of a fake background, a beach with breaking surf in the distance and palm trees waving aloft.

How pathetic.

Most likely, he was in an adjoining room, monitoring a bank of CCTV monitors.

"I'm sorry, Cass," he said. "But someone had to tell you." It was the first time she'd heard his voice, but it didn't bring his identity to mind.

"And you're the Good Samaritan who stepped up to the plate. How noble you are." Cass stared at the screen with all the malice she could muster. She wanted to curse him out. She had curses aplenty. They were lining up, jostling to be the first out of her mouth, and saying them would have felt great. But venting with cuss words was hardly an effective use of her energy. What would he do? Let her go? Say sorry? Ironically, that was exactly what he did say.

"I'm sorry about everything. It wasn't meant to go like that. I didn't know that stuff would make you sick. It made your heart beat fast too. So I had to inject you. Just a little Valium to calm you down."

"You sadistic bastard, why did you show me that?"

"You wouldn't have believed me otherwise. You'd say it was fake. But I'll tell you the hotel they were in if you want. It was one of their favorites, handy for the office."

"You disgusting pervert."

"I never touched you. I'm not an animal."

"Really. From where I'm sitting, you're a shitty pig masquerading as a human being."

"All right, I knew this was coming. Get it off your chest. Let's get it over with."

"What do you want?"

"Plenty of time for that. I put some painkillers on the bottom tray there. Sort yourself out. Have another cup of coffee. It's your favorite. Remind you of that trip to Jamaica with you know who."

Cass studied him. He was playing a game. Jamaica. Yes, with Rob, back in the honeymoon-heat days after they'd met, a quick hop on his private jet, wooing her all the way.

"Do you think my husband is going to pay?"

"He's not your husband. And he never will be."

Cass shifted uncomfortably. Rob had kicked their wedding day back twice. She'd been wondering about that even before the arrival of the anonymous photo.

"So, you tell me my husband's a cheat, and what? You expect me to say thank you?"

"I don't expect anything. Except you give me a chance."

"What sort of chance?" Cass went to the trolley. His invitation to drink another cup of coffee was one she could live with. She sweetened this cup with brown sugar and gulped a mouthful, staring up at his face. He was so ordinary. His lank black hair made her think of dandruff, although she couldn't see any, his pocked skin was so pale he'd be a shoo-in at a vampire convention, and his spongy nose reminded her of something she'd seen growing in a coral reef in the Caribbean. He had a face you'd never forget, but conversely, could never remember. This was her kidnapper, the Antichrist of male charm, a man your subconscious worked overtime to wipe from your memory banks.

"Just get to know me. That's all I ask."

No answer to that one, but plenty of confusion.

Get to know me?

Know?

Was that the biblical *know*, as in, when Adam *knew* Eve, he stuck his cock in her.

"If you're lucky, the police will get to you before Rob. But you don't look lucky to me. Rob heard me. I can't place your hideous face, but he will. He'll track you down. He'll find you, and he'll smash you against a wall until you squirt blood, and I'll watch it all laughing and goading him on."

She finished her coffee and put down the empty cup, feeling better, and it was not just the caffeine. That sex tape had cowed her, beating her down in a corner. But fighting back had bucked her up, the controlled coldness and meanness in her voice strengthening her resolve. She knew who she was and what she was capable of. Now all she needed was a demo, something to rid him of that supercilious sneer. She picked up the tray. Sandwiches, neat and pretty, and scones with cream and jam. Yummy. She hadn't even noticed the scones. Too bad. She lifted the tray to her face and inspected it, sniffing in its flavors, the aftermath of the chemical rag giving way to the tang of fine cheeses. Lovely porcelain too, classy, like the rest of this place.

She raised the tray towards the TV as if offering him a sandwich, then upended it and slammed it down, smashing its contents between the tray and the dresser and spraying bits of china and food fragments all over the floor. Not yet done, she took a second shot at it, lifting the tray two-handed above her head and crashing it down on the remains of her handiwork, shattering his precious porcelain and pulping his meticulously prepared food into goo. Satisfied, she glared up at him, adding a twisted grin to finish the performance.

So what did that achieve?

The question floated around somewhere in the back of her head. The answer was nothing. But she left the question where it was, hidden behind a wall of anger. Sometimes reason is a stumbling block and this was a moment to let her feelings rip. Her captor looked down on her impassively.

"Why don't you take a bath and change? Relax a bit. So you can—"

"Put on a peep show. Isn't that what you mean? Strip off and lather up in the bathroom so you'll have some video to share with your creepy buddies."

"There's no cameras in the bathroom. I swear. And none in the dressing room. I'm not kidding. I wouldn't do that. I admit there's cameras everywhere else. There has to be. I have to keep my eye on you for a while. That's obvious. But not the bathroom. That's private stuff."

Cass turned away and walked to the bathroom. The lying creep didn't deserve an answer. Whether or not he was watching her, she needed a shower. It was only when she reached the door that she noticed she was still holding the tray. She spun midstride like a discus thrower and hurled it at the TV. But Toadface was gone already, the screen blank. Cass stared at it, grinding her teeth, rage a hammering heat in her chest.

6

Sharpe lounged in a black gaming chair so big it dwarfed him, its red piping framing his head and shoulders. The great thing about the gaming chair, apart from it being comfortable enough to live in, was the swivel. Just a kick on the stone floor and he could switch walls, go from the big screen to the wall of monitors. From here, he could see everything happening in the apartment and taking place outside too via the exterior CCTV cameras. So there was a lot of comfort to be had. And when he needed detail, one kick the other way and he had the feed he wanted puffed up to home movie theater size. Yes, the gaming chair was his throne and the control room was his court. But the king of all he surveyed was troubled.

What to do?

His eyes were locked on the big screen.

Cass.

She was sitting on the bed, staring at... what?

He couldn't make that out, some blank spot, maybe nowhere, maybe those scary blue eyes were turned inside out, scanning the thoughts in her head.

So what were they seeing?

His phone buzzed.

Cyclops, his surveillance server, was giving him a shout. He hadn't logged in for more than six hours, and it was set up to remind him if new recordings were piling up. He logged in and got to work.

Washington's phone, currently geolocated in Pix's Notting Hill flat, was an obvious first port of call. He'd called Monty from there. Sharpe played the recording.

"I found out who did it." Washington's opening statement had Sharpe lurching to the edge of his seat, his mind racing. *He knows already? How? Cass and that damn phone call. I know him... from the office. Surely he can't have already—* "I went back to the house today and checked with the security guard who takes care of our neighbor's place."

Sharpe remembered the house on the other side of the alleyway.

"The Arab?"

"Yeah, but he's never there. So I got talking to the guard who drives by a couple of times a day."

"They've got a booth, right? Next to the gate."

"A guardhouse. There's never anyone in it. But they have a fantastic camera set up. So he showed me the footage from yesterday evening."

"That was nice of him."

"Well, not exactly nice. I paid him a small fee for demoing his company's camera system. Wink-wink. Anyway, it caught a van with Fritillary Fields, Gardening Services written on it."

"That's great. So tell the cops. They can take it from there."

"Turns out there's no such company. I checked it at Companies House. Doesn't exist. All fake."

Sharpe chuckled.

Surprise! It was a stencil, you dummy.

There was a long pause after that with Monty finally getting his thoughts together.

"So it wasn't random, him taking her. She was targeted and it was super-planned. A fake company name... that's wild. What was it called again?"

"Fritillary Fields."

"What's that mean?"

"Fritillary is a type of flower or butterfly."

"That's so weird. And a fake address?"

"Of course... telephone number too. It was planned like a military op."

"Scary."

"But I got something. Two things, in fact. He was wearing a Rolex."

Sharpe snapped forward, his smile wiped clean, hands on the desk like a sprinter waiting for the gun.

"A kidnapper with a Rolex!"

Sharpe looked down at his wrist and hurriedly undid the clasp.

"And not just any bloody Rolex, a Daytona. I blew it up. You can see the tach scale. 18 karat Everose gold."

"So who do you have at the office who—"

"No one. We don't pay people that kind of money. I asked Pix. She couldn't think of anyone either. So I told her to get me a list from HR—all the employees who've ever worked there. We'll work through it and maybe it will jog our memories."

"Are you there now? Pix's place."

"I can't stay in Cobham. After what happened in that house—"

"Bad memories? Or are you just avoiding that detective?"

"I told you that's nothing. Anyway, it doesn't matter where I am. When the guy calls with a ransom request, I can take care of it from here as easily as anywhere, and I don't need cops making it complicated and risking her life."

"You think a guy with a collector's dream Rolex is going to want money?"

"What else?"

"Are you pulling my leg? Are we still talking about Cass? You don't know how lucky you are, mate."

"If it was sex, they'd get someone easier. She was targeted. No one sets up an operation like that—with all that risk—just for sex. It has to be money. Maybe this is a full-time job for him. That's how he can afford the watch. Kidnapping the rich is a major industry in some countries. Why not here?"

"It's a shitty thing to do anyway."

"Kidnapping?"

"No, I mean shacking up with your girlfriend while Cass is—"

"I've got no choice. I can't fill in the blanks now, but—"

"Pix is a bitch."

"You've never liked her."

"That's because she's a—"

"Don't even say it!"

"I wouldn't be your friend if I didn't."

"I gotta go."

Sharpe heard a door opening and background noises. He checked the timestamp on the call. 6:30. That had to be Pix arriving home from the office. He stared at his watch, now lying abandoned on the desk. How could he have been so stupid as to wear that?

Stupid analog junk.

With so many great digital watches around, why did he even buy it? That damn movie. He couldn't remember its name, Glengarry something, but who could forget that line, *You see this watch... This watch costs more than your car... that's who I am, and you're nothing.* Yes, sir, at forty thousand dollars, that kind of cool was cheap at the price. But no one had even noticed it until now... until this mega giga cockup.

How had it happened?

His overalls had reached down to his gloved hands, so...?

When I carried her.

His sleeve had slid up his arm, and the neighbor's camera must have caught it for a split second as he'd walked out of the alley.

"I got the van's registration," Washington said with hushed urgency, his voice dragging Sharpe back into the call. "You know guys who can check that. Connections. If they can get me the address—"

"Connections? Like Don Corleone?"

"Come on, Monty. I need to find out who owns that van. You want me to find Cass, don't you?"

"Why are you whispering? What's going on?"

"Pix is back. I don't want her knowing too much."

"You haven't told her?"

"I don't have time for this. I need your help. I stepped up when you needed me, didn't I?"

"Hey, okay... but even if I knew someone, it's not a favor I could ask. And anyway, if the company name and address are fake, then the plate's probably fake too."

"One bitcoin. Maybe it's fake, maybe it's not. But you get one bitcoin for finding out. Last time I looked that was thirty thousand dollars and change. You don't have to ask anyone for favors. Spread money around."

"What's the number? I'll see what I can do."

Sharpe tuned out of the exchange, his eyes on Cass as she stood up and approached the big screen. She said something, but the sound was muted. He quit the call and turned on the two-way audio just in time to hear her say,

"Hey... asshole."

"I'm here," he said, biting his tongue the moment the words left his mouth. Why did he answer? He should have—

"Let's talk."

"And by the way, my name is not arsehole."

"Well... you sure fooled me on that one."

"It's Edward Sharpe. Ted for short. But you can call me Teddy."

"Why? Is that what your friends call you? I mean, if you had any friends."

"All right, call me what you want."

"Thanks, Toady, I will. And now we know each other better, let's talk."

"Go ahead."

"Down here."

"In person?" He wasn't so sure about that. Looking at it one way, it was good. She wanted engagement. But looking at the broken plates and cups on the floor, only an idiot would not think twice.

"If you come, I promise I won't break anything else and that includes you. If you don't come, I'll smash every breakable thing in my charming new home. How's that sound?"

A few choice words came to mind, but Ted set them aside.

"Okay, I'll be there."

He took a holstered baton from the desk drawer, left the control room and went into the apartment. Cass was still in the bedroom when he got there, sitting on the end of the bed.

"Please don't make me use this," he said, waving the ugly black baton. It was shaped like a truncheon, ribbed and bulbous with two shiny spikes at the end. He clicked his thumb and an electric arc crackled menacingly between them, leaving a faint burned taint to the air. He was standing in the doorway, rooted to the spot by her defiant eyes daring him to use it. He took a step closer, lowering the baton and taking care not to step on what remained of the sandwiches. "I'm sorry for hurting you. I'll keep saying sorry until you believe me."

Cass stared at him, eyes wide and angry, body tense.

"This is your new home now," he continued. "Try to understand that. There's no point in smashing it. You have to live in it." He gestured to the shards of porcelain and bits of food scattered between them. "I'll clean this up. I understand you're angry. That's okay. It's normal. I've made you some more food and coffee too. It's upstairs. I'll get it in a minute. You can smash that too if you want. But I'll only clean it up again and bring you more, so why bother? Sooner or later, you'll get it out of your system. You'll understand I don't want to hurt you. Quite the opposite." He was getting through. It was written on her face. Sincerity was working. All he had to do was be nice and he'd wear her down. He lowered his voice. "Have a cup of coffee, eat something."

"I'm not hungry."

"Sure you are. Must be. You're so wound up you can't feel it." He waved the baton at her bathroom. "Like I said, there's no cameras in there. I promise you. Why don't you shower and change your clothes? You'll feel better then." He waited, but she said nothing, her eyes never wavering from his. "You might as well. I'm going to put this away now. Look...." He slid the baton into the holster on his hip. "I'll clean this mess up and bring you more food."

When she made no response, he left the bedroom and went to the kitchenette off the dining area and double-checked the drawers and cupboards. No makeshift weapons. He knew that already, of course. He'd made sure of it. Unlike the other rooms, which were all oversized and equipped with every conceivable feature, the kitchen was minimal, its cooking facilities good for little more than zapping prepared food in a microwave. Its fridge was stocked with drinks and snacks, and its cupboards and drawers equipped with crockery and utensils, the latter all plastic. This was a kitchen built from the getgo for a prisoner. But after her tray-smashing temper tantrum, he needed the reassurance of a double check. If he'd overlooked a knife, he'd be wearing it between his shoulder blades sometime soon. Satisfied, he took a broom and dustpan from the cupboard and went back to the bedroom.

Cass was gone. The bathroom door was closed and running water swished from beyond it. He set to work, sweeping the broken plates and the mulched remains of sandwiches into the dustpan. He dumped it all in a trash bag and fetched a pail of soapy hot water and a mop to finish the job. She was in the shower now, he thought, as he listened to the rush of water coming from the bathroom. He finished the cleanup on his hands and knees, drying the wooden floor with a cloth, smiling feebly. It had been a rocky start. Nothing like the plan. But that sound was comforting. Cass was in the next room doing an everyday thing, taking a shower. He hurried the last of his work and left. He didn't want to be there when she came out. She needed time to explore her new home. He did wonder why she'd summoned him. Their exchange had been so tense she hadn't mentioned it. *Whatever*. She could tell him when she was calm and collected.

He stuck the trash bag on the trolley and wheeled it back upstairs to the farmhouse kitchen where he dumped it and cleaned up the trays. Working at a long wooden table, he loaded the trays with fresh sandwiches and coffee. There was a TV on the wall, squeezed under the kitchen's twisted wooden beams. He flicked his eyes up at it every few seconds, hoping to catch sight of Cass when she emerged from the bathroom. That shower was taking forever. He was almost at the door when he saw her. He spun around to get a better look, his trolley forgotten. She was wearing a saffron toweling bathrobe with her initials monogrammed in black, and—his face broke into a grin—the Versace slippers. She was actually wearing them. *The Butterflies Slippers*. That was what the store had called them. They were black with white polka dots and had butterflies and ladybirds sprinkled between the dots. Two hundred pounds they'd cost him. But he'd have paid two thousand for the sight of her wearing them.

He hurried out of the kitchen, thoughts zigzagging excitedly. He wanted to tell her how happy he was to see her in those slippers, how it was another sign that this was the right thing to do. He wanted to tell her everything, about every turn in the long trail that had brought them together, about *The Collector*, about kismet, chance and fate. But he pulled himself up short at the top of the ramp leading down to the basement. Not yet. It was too soon. He'd tell her. For sure, he would. Cass was his girl now. She had to know the whole story and one day she would, but before then there was plenty of growing to do, growing together, becoming one. He left the food cart by the table in the dining room and went through to the bedroom.

"Cass."

There was no sign of her, and the bathroom door was open and its lights were off. She had to be in the camera-free dressing room. He went back to the dining area off the living room, planning to lay out the food and exit quietly. But as he was laying it out, she came up behind him.

"What do you want with me?" she said.

He whirled around, snatching the baton off the tray. Her eyes flashed on it and he regretted his defensive reflex. He didn't want to threaten her. She seemed calmer now. That was why she'd called him. She had a question. She wanted to know. He let the baton fall to his side, his expression softening.

"In the beginning, I just want to be your friend," he said. "Right now, I'm a stranger to you. I get it. I'm that horrible man who kidnapped you, who got rough with you. You're angry. It's normal. But once you get to know me, you'll realize I'm a good person, a kind person. And there's everything you could want here. Swimming pools, indoor and outdoor, a tennis court, I've got a games room that's eye-popping, every video game on the planet and a wonderful movie theater."

"And that's supposed to make me like you?" He didn't answer. This conversation was going wrong already. He was stoking her anger, not calming it. "If so, it's not working. I hate you!"

"You don't know me. I'm a much better person than Rob Washington. He's a scumbag, a whore. He's not worthy of you." Cass didn't react other than with that stare, bristling blades of hate. But there had to be more going on inside her head, he thought. She had to be wondering how he knew so much about her. "Why don't you pour yourself some coffee?"

She looked at the fine table he'd laid out, then after a pause, she poured a cup of coffee and sipped it.

Good.

It wasn't much in the way of progress—his suggestion, her acceptance—but he pocketed it like a winner's medal. She picked up a sandwich, scrutinized it and pecked at it as she walked to the end of the table and sat down.

"So you've been stalking me?"

"I don't like that word. I've been observing you, finding out everything I could about you. I've done it all in the background or online, making sure I wouldn't upset or frighten you."

"Until you attacked me in my home, beat me up, chloroformed me, and kidnapped me." She checked out her sandwich, easing up the bread with her fingertips to check the contents. He wanted to tell her about the cheese, the salmon and cucumber—all her favorites—but he kept quiet, hoping she'd eat it. "I'd say you were making up for lost time and doing a pretty good job of it."

"It wasn't chloroform. It was—"

"I don't give a damn what it was. It made me sick, you pig." She tasted the sandwich, a nibble. Maybe the food will improve her mood, he thought, but he wasn't optimistic. Something was wrong. She was too quiet too soon after that explosion of anger. There was something odd about that. *Tick-tock*. He could hear it ticking away inside her, not sure what, but something built to go bang. The moments clicked off, Ted waiting apprehensively and getting ready to duck. "Nice sandwiches." She took another.

A compliment?

Tick-tock.

His inner voice was screaming, *Duck now*! But he couldn't stop himself from saying, "Thank you."

"Why did you send me the photo?"

"No reason. No plan."

"Softening me up... was that the idea?"

"I did it on a whim."

"Taking me wasn't a whim." She nibbled her new sandwich. "All this..." She waved it around, meaning the underground apartment he'd built.

"Two years. Full-time, more or less."

"I should be flattered. That's a lot of work and a ton of money."

"You're worth it, Cass. Every moment, every penny."

"So it's not money you want. I've figured that much out. What then?... Sex? You could have had me when I was knocked out. Or don't you like girls who play dead? Odd that. You look the type."

"Type?"

"What do they call you guys?" Cass put down her half-eaten sandwich and frowned. "Incels. That's it. Involuntary celibates. I can smell it on you."

"I'm not an incel." He took half a step towards her, his body stiffening.

"Sure you are. What's this"—she rolled her eyes and waved her arms—"this situation? If this isn't coercion, if this isn't—what do feminists call it?—enforced monogamy under strict patriarchal rules, then what is it?"

"I never touched you."

"Not yet... but how future-proof is that promise? What was it you said? In the beginning, we'll be friends. My takeaway from that is... you're an incel. Maybe secretly as in secret even from yourself. An incel stuck in his own jail."

"I'm not a prisoner. I can—"

"Up here, pal." She tapped her head. "No bars in your jail, just walls of delusion. You think you're a nice guy, right? Well, here's the news. Nice guys don't grab women out of their homes or anywhere else. Nice guys don't have rape fantasies period, and only an incel whose brain had derailed would hide his sicko dream even from himself. So what's your story? Been reading too many fairy tales? Is that where our friendship is going to end up? True love."

She stood up, slapping her hands together as if brushing crumbs off them. Her sudden movement spooked him and he took a step back.

"What is it creeps like you call women like me...? Stacy. That's it. We're Stacys in your world." She ran her hands from her hips up to her breasts and back down across her belly to her thighs. "Am I what you've always dreamed of, an alpha bitch who doesn't even see a little toad like you, who only gives it up to a guy like Rob, a drop-dead gorgeous hunk with a body like a Greek god and an undercarriage like a Derby Champion."

She worked her hands on her body again, sliding them up to her breasts and giving them a coquettish boost. She held them there, swiveling her body and tilting her butt just so.

"Stop it! I'm not a creep. I hate that dirty talk. Act properly. I hate those groups. All they talk about is—"

"A reformed incel? You abandoned your brothers? Oh, no sweetie... you made a mistake. You can take the boy out of the club, but you can't take the club out of the boy. You're hardcore incel." She took a step closer, leaned forward and sniffed. "Definitely." He wanted to back off, but he was nailed to the spot. He had the stun gun. He was in control. He was in the driver's seat. But she was giving him the old heave-ho and grabbing the steering wheel. "So this is your pathetic attempt to turn a true love fantasy into reality? You stole a real-life Stacy. You finally own one. But nothing's changed. There's still only one alpha in the room and that's me, and you're just the little shit who cleans up my mess—"

He hit her, not too hard. A slap. But hard enough. She stumbled back and grabbed the table to catch herself.

He was quaking.

Where did that...? How did that...?

He had no answers. It had come from somewhere else, maybe even someone else. He would never hit her. He would never...

"I'm sorry. I'm so sorry. I had to stop you." He stepped back, watching her as she pulled herself up straight, horribly calm.

She went behind a chair at the end of the table and leaned on it, panting, but not desperate, not like a wounded animal, more like a lioness with her eyes on the prey.

"Methinks I hit the spot."

Ted was looking one way, then the other, anywhere but at her.

"I'd never hurt you. I love you. I did all this for... I wanted us to have a chance. To get to know each other so..." He stepped towards her, appealing.

"Get back." She twisted the chair around, blocking his path.

"No, no." He held up his arms, noticing the baton for the first time. He stepped back. "I'd never hurt you."

"Oh, really." She touched her cheek. "That's not what it felt like."

Ted whined, turning away, tossing from side to side like a puppet with a crazy master.

"I never would, I—"

"Fuck off, liar."

Ted stopped his tossing and turning, his whining and pleading. He looked down at the baton long and hard, then fired it up, holding it like a candle burning in front of his face. He stared at her defiantly, then slammed its sparking point into his thigh and screamed.

7

Cass yelped as Ted stumbled back and hit the wall. She crouched behind the chair, flinching, trying to make sense of it.

He zapped himself.

She hadn't seen that coming. She'd watched him writhing on the spot, twisting this way and that. Then he'd sparked up the stun gun and held it up like a sacred candle at a black magic mass. Right then, she'd known what was coming and it was going to hurt. She'd pushed him too far and he'd flipped. Now she'd pay the price for shooting off her mouth, and the price was pain measured in millions of volts. Sure enough, he flipped. Something inside him snapped and the cables that wired him together went into meltdown.

Bham!

But he'd picked up the check himself. He'd paid the pain price in full on her behalf.

Cass held on to the back of the chair, skin stretched white across her knuckles, anything to stop her hands from shaking, anything to anchor her trembling body.

Ted slid down the wall, the baton falling from his hand. It crossed her mind to grab it. She could dance around the table and snatch it up. Maybe she'd get to it first. Maybe, maybe, maybe. It was just a dream, not even that, a whim that flitted through her head and got shooed away by terror. She'd had plenty to fear in the past forty-eight hours, but nothing like this. He'd taken the physical pain, but the emotional hit was on her. In a stroke, he'd demoed how crazy he was. A dozen psychiatrists could have delivered the verdict in a thousand-page dissertation. But that would have been far less convincing. If he was method-acting madness, he'd just earned himself an Oscar.

That could have been you.

The words ran on an endless tape inside her head.

Wake up!

She'd been saved by what? It hurt her to think it, but it had to be love. It was the only thing that made sense, his twisted take on love. But what twisted one way could easily twist the other. This guy was deranged in the most dangerous of ways. By any definition, he was off-the-wall crazy, but he believed he was a nice guy, and between these two Teds was a gaping crevasse with monsters fighting in its depths.

What were you thinking?

She had no answer.

His apologies? Was that it?

He kept saying sorry. He'd doped her into cocky arrogance by saying it ten-thousand times. So when she'd stumbled on his sore spot, she'd poked it with a stick for no other reason than it felt good.

He was on the ground propped up against the wall, still in a semiconscious fug with spit dribbling from his mouth. His eyes were open but glazed. That zap hadn't knocked him unconscious, but it must have hurt like hell. Her thoughts went back to the baton and she measured the distance from his hand to the weapon with her eyes. Just inches. So now her shakes were calming, she wondered, *could I make it*? His fingers answered her, crawling towards it spiderlike. Cass pulled herself together, taking deep breaths. He wasn't going to hurt her now. But she'd have to wise up. No more goading, no more poking that incel sore. That was a no go area.

So what's the new plan?

Make nice and kill time was all she could think of. The cops had to be on the way. She had to hold out, keep him off the boil, warm, but not hot. He got to his feet, sliding his back up the wall. His face was sheet white, his eyes black dots in red saucers. He stood stock still, belly and chest pumping in and out like wheezy bellows. Cass stared motionless, still holding the chair, but relaxed now, prepping her make-nice game face. He pushed himself off the wall unsteadily and holstered the baton.

"You won't believe this, but"—he sucked in a breath—"I planned a welcome dinner for you later. I already ordered the stuff in from a posh French restaurant."

Cass waited for him to go on, but he seemed to want some comment from her.

"That's thoughtful," she said, snipping the word surreal out of her reply in a last-minute edit.

"Should I cancel it?"

He looked at her squarely. He'd been avoiding eye contact since the zapping. But now she'd said something nice, he was running with it.

"We have to eat... and I love French food."

"8 o'clock?"

She nodded. He went to go but turned back.

"Can we forget this?" He waited, hope in his eyes. Cass was losing her place. It was hard to process it all and make sense of it. This guy was half Bambi and half Hannibal Lecter.

"People lose their temper. It's only human. This isn't easy for either of us, but..." She signed off on it with a shrug.

He nodded, walked towards the door, then turned once more. "I'm going to put on a suit and tie. Like it's a proper date."

Cass forced a smile. This was getting harder and harder. She wanted to scream, but said, "See you at eight."

As soon as she was alone, she hurried to the bathroom, shut the door and sat on the floor with her back to it, her elbows on her knees and her face buried in her hands. She sat like that, letting her head clear and her turbulent emotions settle. It took hours, or maybe that was just how long it felt. She walked around the apartment after that. She'd already explored the place, so this was stretching her legs. She peeked in a few drawers and cupboards she'd missed the first time around, finding a yoga mat. She rolled it out on the floor at the end of the bed. If ever she'd needed a de-stress session, this was it. She lay on her back in the corpse pose, letting her arms and legs flop out to the side. She thought about the dinner, how to frame the upcoming conversation. She had to be smart, not stupid, never saying anything that didn't track back to her end goal—getting out of this place. The mat underneath her was thick and felt good. She wriggled into its comfort, her arms stretching out to the side until—

What's that?

Her arm had inadvertently slid under the bed and she'd touched something.

She gasped a sharp breath.

Whatever it was, it had cut her finger.

She pulled her hand away from it and rubbed her fingers together.

Blood... just a little.

Thank God she hadn't grabbed it.

But what was it?

She stood up, folding her hand into a gentle fist to conceal the blood from the cameras, and went to the bathroom. It was a scratch on the thumb. She ran cold water on it and dabbed it with tissue paper until it stopped bleeding. Porcelain. It had to be the remains of a plate. Ted hadn't cleaned under the bed, and a fragment of china must have skidded there. How fortunate. And how lucky she was to cut herself. If she hadn't, the idea might not have come to her. But now it was obvious. If it could cut her, it could cut him. And if it was sharp enough to cut her after a casual touch like that, it might make a serious weapon. Whatever it was, she had to get it out from under the bed in full view of the cameras without raising any suspicions.

But what would she use it for? Defense or offense? Should she stash it ready for the day—and she was sure it would come—when he laid into her, ripping her clothes off? Or should she go on the offensive as part of an escape plan? On the other side of *make nice and wait to be rescued* was *who knows where this will go tomorrow*? But how would offense work in practice? And what if she killed him, how would she get out of the basement?

With no clear plan, she kicked the whys and wherefores down the road. The immediate priority was getting her hands on it. All the rest could be figured out later. She flushed the toilet, then took a towel back into the bedroom. She rolled it tight and set it on the yoga mat as she lay down, fitting it under her neck like a cervical pillow.

Now, didn't that look natural?

Comfortable, too. She closed her eyes and stretched her arms, feeling her way gingerly under the bed, nails first to make contact without cutting herself again. So far, so good. She fixed its location in her head and waited twenty minutes, long enough to fake a meditation session and for him to get bored should he be watching, although she doubted that. After that freak show, he had to be way too shaken up to enjoy a Big Brother episode. He'd be licking his wounds somewhere, staring at good-sized burn holes in his thigh and wondering how he could have been that stupid. She pulled herself up, unwound her cervical pillow and spread the towel horizontally, making a cross with the yoga mat and tucking the end of the towel under the bed. She sat on the towel and did some simple asanas, stretching out after her meditation. Then she gathered up the towel, taking care to snaffle up the plate fragment without cutting herself, and went to the bathroom.

The moment of truth.

Was the bathroom really free of cameras?

Or was Ted a liar?

She was about to find out. Earlier, the prospect of him spying on her naked body had not troubled her much. She'd sunbathed topless on beaches throughout Europe and gone totally naked on more than a few. Given the issues at stake, Ted enjoying a peep show was not a fight worth taking on. But this? Fashioning a shard of china into a knife. If he was watching, she'd soon know about it.

Only one way to find out.

Cass unfolded the towel, her eyes gobbling up the prize.

Perfect.

A bit of a plate, yes, but not a weedy chip; this was a blade. It was long and sharp, and no ordinary porcelain either, but rock-hard, wafer-thin bone china. Holding it with a towel, she sliced strips off a face cloth, then wound them around the thick end of it to make a handle and tied the cloth on tight with dental floss.

Ferrying her towel with its hidden cargo past the cameras to the dressing room, she cut a strip of cloth off a blouse and fashioned an improvised sheath inside her thigh. The knife was a game changer. At a stroke, her make-nice plan was jettisoned. That was a survival agenda, but it didn't help her escape. His raging mania was now clear and that made a prison breakout the best option. She'd also figured out how to go on the offensive and survive. Killing him was off the table. She'd still be locked in. She'd die in his five-star jail watching him rot. But what if she half-killed him, sliced into an artery? There was one in the thigh, the femoral artery. What if she cut it? Her brother had taught her stuff like this. Fresh back from his first tour of duty in Afghanistan, Josh had drilled her in knife fighting, unarmed combat and survival tactics. Not that their neighborhood was as rough as Helmand province, but protecting his kid sister had been second only in importance to serving his country.

She winced inside, that twist in the gut that always found her when Josh came to mind. She let it go. He'd taught her that too. *Can't change it, let it go. Can change it, do it*. Her focus back on Toady, the plan rolled out before her. He'd live if she cut him right. Then she'd offer to call A & E. Emergency services, they called it in England, not 911, but 999. All he had to do was give her his phone. His choice would be simple, game over or life over. Or she could drive him to the hospital. He might die on the way, of course, in which case, *boo-hoo*. Either way, he'd be a goner without her.

So that was the new plan, make nice giving way to make nasty. It could work and there were only two ways it could go wrong. She could overdo it and end up locked in a basement with a dead man, or underdo it and... what then? She sat at her beauty station eyeing herself in the mirror, knife in hand courtesy of Wedgwood, a name she'd come across at the Royal Academy, a potter famous for his pale blue and white Jasperware, famous too for his campaign against the slave trade. A fitting accomplice. Cass was a captive slave, albeit a pampered one, and this gleaming spike and her brother's Marine Corps training were going to set her free.

8

Ted was sitting on a stool in his bathroom, the nasty word floating around in his head too. He was staring at the burns on his thigh. His thick denim jeans had offered some protection. But those sparking steel teeth had burned through them, singeing two spots about a centimeter apart, red dots ringed by a black and purple bruise, like two bullseyes on a fancy dartboard.

Damn, it hurt.

He held a bag of ice against it until it went numb, then rubbed it with Vaseline. That was the best he could do. He checked the time on his phone, his abandoned watch still sitting on the desk in the control room.

Plenty of time to get ready.

He dried his leg, put his pants back on and checked the apartment via the CCTV app on his phone. No sign of Cass. She had to be in the bathroom or the dressing room getting ready. At moments like this, he regretted his decision not to put cameras in either of those locations. But no, it had been the right thing to do. He wasn't a Peeping Tom, despite her horrible accusations. *Incel.* How could she say that? She didn't even know him. And what a repulsive word. Incel. It sounded like a worm that wriggled its way out of rotting flesh. The image made him shudder. She'd soon see. She'd learn the truth about him, and the first step down that road was learning the truth about Rob Washington, the whole truth.

He left the bathroom, sat on his bed and turned on the TV.

6 o'clock news.

The usual, the war in Europe, the latest government cock-ups, climate disasters—we're all going to die. He waited. No mention of Cass. News segued into sports, and while that played out in the background, he checked news outlets and social media on his phone, searching and searching. There was nothing. No mention of anybody being abducted anywhere. If it was out there, this story would be big. Cass was not a drunken teenager grabbed on her way home from a nightclub at 4 a.m.. She was a woman abducted from her own home in one of the wealthiest neighborhoods in the country. Her partner was a rich man with a rich man's access to people in high places as well as the media. And yet there was nothing. Having eavesdropped on Washington's conversation with Monty, Ted was expecting this, but not counting on it. Washington could have changed his mind, taken the advice of his old friend and called the police. But he hadn't.

Ted slid off the bed and showered, then washed his hair and shaved, cooling his face afterward with a French antiaging cream. He'd only been using it for a few weeks, but he was convinced it was working. He'd gotten a few tips on personal grooming from the fashionista he'd hired to buy Cass's clothes. Some of it made no sense to him, but he took it as gospel and followed her rules anyway. He donned a white shirt and a light blue suit made of a silk and linen blend. Italian, all the way from Milan. He slipped on Gucci suede moccasins over white cotton socks and admired himself in the full-length mirror. Amazing. He was a new man. The pricey Italian threads worked like a Superman outfit, transforming the innocuous Clark Kent into.... No, not Clark Kent. What was John Travolta's name in that movie? He couldn't remember. But he struck the pose anyway and sang a few bars of

Stayin Alive until he ran out of lyrics. He pulled himself up straight and took a deep breath.

Super Ted.

What woman could resist me now?

He smiled and scored the result from one to ten.

Not good. It rated a four and that was being generous. Once, twice, three times. He finally got a smile that didn't look too creepy and took it downstairs with the afterburn of *Staying Alive* putting a spring in his steps. In the kitchen, he prepared a trolley, not the cute round one he'd used earlier, but a big one like the food cart they use in a posh steakhouse to serve up Châteaubriand. When the food arrived, he laid everything out nicely, wheeled it down to the basement, and stopped at the apartment door. He didn't want to show up before she was ready—last minute jitters on date night. So he whipped out his phone and checked how she was doing via CCTV.

Cass.

He gasped.

She was stepping out of her dressing room, looking not just beautiful, but perfect. What was it? What had she done to herself? Was it the makeup? The hair? Or was it that black dress? No. It wasn't any of that. No one thing. It was the whole thing. Cass. She was everything a woman could be to a man, and the sight of her swept aside that throb of pain inside his thigh and banished his nerves.

She's done it all for me. She finally realizes....

It was that zapping, he thought. *By punishing myself for slapping her, I've convinced her. She finally understands how much I love her*. Nursing his wound, it had seemed so stupid. But pride surged in him now. Sometimes, crazy was the right thing.

Talk lies. Action is truth.

The door opened with a pneumatic wheeze. He pushed the trolley through and it closed automatically behind him.

"Teddy's here."

She didn't answer, but distant sounds of movement told him she would soon join him. He laid the food out on the dining room table, transferring it dish by dish. No Châteaubriand, no chunky steaks requiring a steak knife, only items that could be cut easily by an innocuous roundheaded table knife with a gently serrated edge. That was important. The stun baton was nowhere to be seen, but he wasn't entirely defenseless with pepper spray in his jacket pocket and a mini stun gun disguised as a pen tucked in his inside pocket. She had to believe he trusted her, although in truth, he was a long way from that. The door opened and she peeked around it, smiling before stepping into the room and swirling once, her arms outstretched, giving him a good look. Ted's breath caught in his throat. He'd so wanted to act cool, not be star struck like an idiot teenager.

But look at her!

"Good evening," he said, trying to keep his voice from cracking up.

"Ted."

He gestured towards the chair at one end of the table, far enough to be safe but not distant. She nodded and sat down. He scurried around the table with the wine bottle, spewing compliments, all rehearsed and sounding so much better at rehearsals. He poured her a glass of white wine, a Pouilly-Fumé, the Silex cuvée recommended by the restaurant. He poured it slowly, his eyes flashing up at her like a rhythmic beacon. He couldn't help it. The way she held herself, so poised and elegant, despite her predicament. Cass was pure class. Not the class you get from your mum and dad, or a pile of money in your bank account, but class that came from... He didn't know where. Somewhere else. Somewhere he'd never been and would never go. Class he'd never have.

That was okay. He had Cass.

He poured his own glass, and while still standing, tilted it at her like Humphrey Bogart did in some movie.

"New beginnings."

Her eyebrows arched up and a smile creased her cheeks.

"I'll drink to that."

As they worked their way through a seafood salad, Ted steered the conversation toward safe topics. He wanted her to feel comfortable, to let her guard down. But he couldn't shake the nagging feeling she was still on edge, sizing him up, calculating her next move. He had a few calculations running in his head too. There was one topic he wanted to talk about, or if not about at least around. He had to veer their conversation towards it as a minimum. He had to take the risk and that meant pushing his luck.

"You remembered me from the office?"

"Kind of... but not really. Not your name, or anything. It just popped into my head. I knew I'd seen you there, but not when or any of the circumstances. Why? Do you want to tell me?"

"It's not important. I did a bit of contracting there is all. Tell me about your travels. That's much more interesting. Backpacking in Asia right after your parents' accident must have been... Wow, I can't imagine." He tried to sound casual. But that was a deep truth probe guaranteed to give her a jolt. And so it did. She looked up from her plate, eyes narrow and sharp. Ted could almost hear the gears shifting in her head.

"How do you know about that?"

"Social media, I think," he said, backpedaling. He was itching to get to the truth, to tell her everything he knew about her. But this was way too early for the truth, and this was way too pushy. Reminding her he'd been a gold-medal stalker was hardly going to help his case. "I didn't mean to pry. I just wanted to know more about you. I think you mentioned India in one post. Fascinating place." Cass went back to her plate, sorting seafood with her fork and washing down a last shrimp with a sip of wine.

He took care of their empty plates, shuffling around the table, his feigned casualness like a soft mitten on an iron bar. Cat and mouse was a dangerous game to play with Cass. He'd start as the cat. But then the who's who of it would get foggy and the roles recast. "Did you get to see much of it?" he said, looking up from his waiter and busboy chores.

"Goa, of course," she said so quickly it took him by surprise. Her tone was conversational, engaged. Evidently, she'd found the right gear and it was full speed ahead. "Everyone goes there. And Rishikesh, so different and so special."

"What about Manali? Did you go there?" That frown again. And this time she made no effort to hide it. He'd overdone it. Too specific. He should have said up north. "Pondicherry was my favorite place in the whole country." He rambled on, papering over an awkward moment. "Loved the French Quarter."

Ted fiddled with the hotplate on the trolley and busied himself with serving the main course, a handy excuse for avoiding her razorblade eyes. Manali. Surely she'd remember now.

"You were in the Himalayas?" she said.

"Many years ago." He used a napkin to wipe a splash of sauce off the edge of her plate before sliding it in front of her.

"Where did you go?"

"Nowhere you'd know." He served himself—"I was way off the usual backpacking routes."—and sat at the table. "I was looking for an Emperor."

"And did you find one?"

"As a matter of fact, I did." He chuckled. "He's upstairs. I'll introduce you if you like." Cass didn't comment on that. She picked up her fork with the right hand, the way Americans do, and forked a piece of meat. "An Emperor of India. A Kaiser-i-Hind, that's what I was after. It's a butterfly. Super rare and very beautiful. It was in my early days as a collector. I was a fanatic back then. I'd go to any lengths to get what I wanted, and the Emperor was top of my hit list. Actually, the Emperor and his Empress. I wanted a couple. They're sexually dimorphic. The sexes are different, like people. The males are bigger, like us. They're also more brightly colored. That's the opposite of us, I suppose. And the sexes have different habits. Males spend a lot of time looking for a mate and showing off. Territorial displays, they call it. Females, of course, spend their time looking for good places to lay eggs."

"Of course," she said, her face expressionless as she raised her empty red wine glass and chinked it against her empty white wine glass.

"Blimey, here I am going on..." He leaped up and grabbed a bottle of wine from a side table. "Eating yummy beef casserole without red wine... what kind of host am I?" He opened the bottle, yanking the cork when it gave him trouble and slopping wine on the floor. "This was a special year," he said, ignoring the mess. "Or so the man said, the sommelier, wine expert. Cost me three hundred pounds this Bordeaux." He poured their glasses and raised his. "Cheers." He took a gulp. "What do you think?"

Cass sipped once, then twice. She lowered the glass, her steady eyes watching him wait but saying nothing. Then she raised it to her mouth and drained it, licking the last of it off her lips before delivering her verdict.

"And worth every penny."

Ted buzzed inside.

A compliment.

And with that in the bank, he sat down.

Enough cat and mouse, enough India clues. All the pieces of the puzzle were out there now. It was up to her to figure out how they fitted together. The food was a match for the fine wine, and enjoying them, they each kept their own counsel with their conversation hovering around both.

After the main course, Ted cleared the table and suggested they finish the Bordeaux before he served the dessert.

"It's Tarte Tatin with butter pecan ice cream, and I'm serving it with a tawny port, a vintage Colheita. Very special." Ted had no idea what he was talking about, but he was sure he'd gotten it right. Cass shrugged her agreement and picked up her glass. The music stopped and Ted went to his phone as if to cue another playlist, but he stopped as if changing his mind. "Would you like to see the news? You must be dying for a bit of telly."

"Is there something on it you want me to see?"

That was always the problem with Cass. He loved it and he hated it. She was so damn smart. There was no way to slide anything past her, however well it was hidden.

"He didn't report it. Washington. He never called the police. You're not even missing. So far, my crime doesn't exist."

"It does here. Right here in this room."

"So?" He nodded at the TV again, ducking the gauntlet she'd tossed him.

"I'll pass. How do I even know it's for real? You could have edited the real news to make it look like anything. If you can put together all this penitentiary grade security, you could certainly do that."

"What if he tells you in person?"

"Rob?"

Ted topped up her glass and then his own, taking his time about it to keep her on tenterhooks. This was it—the big moment—and it deserved a warm-up act. He picked up his phone and moments later two voices Cass knew well gave her the answer.

"Gone?" Ted had no need to ID the speaker. Cass would recognize Pix's voice wearing earmuffs. "Like the girl in that movie?"

"No." Ted studied the face across the table to catch the moment she heard her cheating man talk about her with his lover. "Gone Girl was faking her disappearance. Cass isn't."

"I don't believe it," Cass said, shaking her head.

Ted snatched up the phone and stopped the audio. He wanted her to hear every word of this.

"Or maybe you refuse to believe it."

"You deepfaked it. How else could you...?" She ran out of words, looking doubtful.

Had she already forgotten the love scene in the hotel? He'd recorded that six months earlier. He had years of this stuff.

"I got an Olympic gold. Not for running or throwing stuff. For maths. Ever heard the word prodigy? I was already at Oxford when other kids were still studying for their GCEs." He waited, thoughtful, then added, "Maybe tenth grade or something in the US. Anyway, I couldn't hack it there. So the government offered me a job. I couldn't hack it there either as it happened. But while I was there, I helped roll out Pegasus. Israeli spyware. Super stuff. Of course, I've got my own version now." He winked, going back to his phone. "I could have faked the voices—it's true—although I didn't. Not believing your ears is smart. But what about your eyes? Take a good look at the location—Pix's flat in Notting Hill. Incidentally, that's where your fine, upstanding fellow has taken up residence since your departure. So how did I fake that?"

Her eyes went up to the screen and the light in them faded. He'd called it right. No way to poker face her way through this one. It was so natural, so obviously not fake. Although it wasn't much of an image, either. At its center was a ceiling. Nothing to see there. But fanning out on either side it got interesting. Rob Washington and his lover were sitting at a table wedged up against a wall in a poky kitchen. Closest to the phone, which appeared to be lying in the middle of the table, was a bottle of red wine. There were two glasses beyond that, and sitting in close was Pix. On the other side, Washington's arm draped down and rested on the table, but the image cut off at his shoulder. Ted switched the audio feed back on, and they picked up the conversation where they'd left it with Pix sounding more like a cop than a lover.

"How do you know she's not faking it? Maybe she's found out about us and wants to stitch you up." Pix snatched up her glass, getting closer to the camera, close enough to see her mouth move. "I've never trusted her. She's—"

"I heard it."

"Heard what?"

"She phoned me while it was happening."

"How could she phone you in the middle of being kidnapped? That's ridiculous. She's working with him.

It's obvious. Maybe he's her lover and they're trying to screw money out of you."

"It sounded real to me."

"What did the police say?" There was a long pause, an empty one. "You didn't call them?"

"The guy said he'd kill her if I did."

"How much did he want?"

"It's not about money. It can't be. There's been no contact."

"You're too trusting. What do you really know about that woman? How come she's got no family?"

"Her mum and dad died in a car crash. I told you."

"But no brothers or sisters, either. And no cousins, uncles or aunts. No friends. She's like a fucking replicant."

"Okay. You two don't get along. I get it."

"This whole thing stinks to me. She's found out about us and this is her payback. She's shacked up with her lover and they're laughing at you. *Let's screw Rob for every penny he's got*. What a brilliant plan!"

Washington came into focus as he leaned forward, elbows on the table, and sipped his wine. "I picked up Italian on the way over," he said, evidently done with that line of conversation.

Ted froze the recording.

"Sorry," he said, "but you had to know."

He watched Cass as she tried to smother her distress, flicking her eyes up at the TV to avoid his. She didn't want him to know he'd won. But he had. A warm glow filled his body. That Siri call, the unexpected disaster, had yielded this unexpected bonus. No police. He couldn't have planned it, but he'd gotten it, and now was the time to press his advantage. He swept his finger back and forth on the phone and pictures scrolled across the TV screen—Pix and Rob in bars, restaurants, parks, cars. They looked like paparazzi shots, taken from a distance or up close with a concealed camera. They weren't necking in all the images, but their body language told the same story in every shot. Her eyes widened and her chest heaved.

She hadn't known, he thought. Not until he'd emailed her that photograph. But even after the hotel sex scene he'd played her on day one, she'd still been unconvinced, unable to accept it, the deep fake excuse coming to his rescue. And he'd sometimes wondered if they'd had an open relationship, although he'd never seen evidence of Cass playing around. But she might have known about Washington's infidelity and chosen to tolerate it. Some women did, some men too. He kept quiet, giving her space to process it all. He had his answer now. The dark look in her eyes, the riddled brow and tight jaw, that was a sworn statement. This was today's headline news, not the abduction of a wealthy woman from her own home, but what a son of a bitch her fiancé was.

Cass looked away and drank her wine, finishing it in two lusty gulps. "Fuck him. Pix is a snake with two heads and he's a worm with no heart. They'll make a great couple." She held up her empty glass. "Let's skip the dessert. But I'll take a shot of that port wine."

Ted killed the screen, not sure where to go next. He'd expected her to break down and burst into tears so he could console her. This performance was meant to crush her spirit. It had hurt her all right. But then she'd killed the pain stone dead. All that heat and anger, she'd just let it go. That was awesome. She'd pulled his red-hot poker out of her belly and stuck it in ice water to turn it blue. She hadn't said the words, but what he'd heard was, So what!

"Good idea. Let's drink to the future and put the past behind us." Ted's heart raced as he hurried over to the drinks trolley. Was that the wine kicking it off?

He wasn't much of a drinker. But no, it was Cass, not the wine. This was even better than the emotional breakdown he'd expected. She'd dumped Washington. She'd dumped that bastard like a piece of trash. She was that strong. He'd done her a favor by showing her those photos and she appreciated it. He opened the wine, and forgetting the port sippers standing next to it, he took it back to the table and poured a healthy measure into her red wine glass. "Your instincts were right about him," he said, his smile irresistibly transformed into a smirk. "He was a serial—"

Ted screamed and tossed the bottle aside. He staggered back and stared at the cloth-handled shard of china sticking out of his blood-soaked thigh. His butt crashed against the food cart and it skittered against the wall. Cass leaped up, her fist clenched around the stem of her glass. Port wine slopped across the table as she smashed the glass on it. Then she reared up in front of him, slashing its jagged edge back and forth. He ducked aside but way too slow, and she caught him, missing his throat, but opening his cheek to the bone. He lost his balance and fell against the wall. He thrust his hand in his pocket as she closed in, arcing the bloodied glass back and forth. He had the pepper spray in his hand. She stabbed at his throat but he dodged to the side, his finger finding the button.

A stream of capsicum foam hit her face and she yelped, dropping the glass and stumbling back. She was blinded, but for how long? And how long had he got? How much blood had he lost? His pant leg was soaked already and blood dribbled down his neck from his face. She came at him, flailing her arms blindly, aiming at whatever was out there. He dodged and slipped behind her, looping his arm around her throat and dragging her back. But he couldn't control her. He lost balance and they both went down, the pepper spray skidding out of reach.

The stun gun.

He pushed her aside and dived into his pocket. Cass struggled to her feet and she was halfway up by the time he had the stun gun out. She wobbled, half-blinded, but still on the attack. He leaped on her and dug the sparking steel barbs into the back of her neck. Right on the spinal cord, it didn't take long. She writhed and jolted. But he held on, his wrist digging into her windpipe and the stun gun shocking the back of her neck. Her body went limp. He crawled to the wall and used it as a crutch to get back on his feet. She was motionless. But how long would that last? He put his hand on his thigh to staunch the blood. The wound was serious. There was a big artery down there, but surely she hadn't got it or he'd be dead already.

He hobbled out of the apartment, went to his control room, and strapped his thigh with a tourniquet made from a belt. Then he staunched the blood flow with adhesive tape. He had to be quick. The Valium was upstairs in his bathroom. He needed to get that and a needle. He'd knock her out good, then drive to the hospital. After this, there was only one way forward. Like any smart geek, Ted always planned for failure. Yes, he had a Plan B. It was gruesome and it was coming.

9

Cass woke with a start, her eyes bleary, her body racked with aches in too many places to count. She groaned when the memory hit her.

Total recall... and all of it ugly.

She rolled over, stifling her groans in the pillow. It would be so easy to cry, to let those fine Egyptian cotton pillowcases soak up the pain. But it would change nothing. There was no forgetting. This was failure with an F so big there was no way to duck it. The only option was to take it on the chin and let it hurt. She rolled onto her back, wide eyes fixed on the ceiling, but watching the slideshow running in her head.

Click-click.

The dinner date from hell played out frame by frame right up to her warrior queen moment and its aftermath—his blood squirting hot and wet on her hand, pepper scorching her eyes, their his-and-hers chorus of screams, and the climax, squirming under him and fading to dark. There was only one positive takeaway in this picture book tale of disaster. She'd had the guts to do it after sitting on the fence for most of the evening, paralyzed by the silent mantra running in her head—*shall I or shan't I?*

The kitchen sink drama clip starring Pix and Rob had been the clincher. Line by line it had pumped white-hot anger up from her belly to her brain and blanked out anything even close to reasoning. If they had been around, she would have stuck her china shiv into both of them, but Toady was the only available candidate. So he'd gotten it. Not that he didn't deserve it. He'd done terrible things to her. He'd triggered a terrible anger in her. But this was different. Rob and

Pix merited an upgrade on anger. They were loathsome, a class apart. Which was the most despicable? Hard to say. Was it Rob for shacking up with his lover the day after his wife was abducted, or was it Pix for celebrating the event by dragging him into her bed within 24 hours?

Cass left the debate, the jury split. She'd come back to it another day and deliver a verdict and a fitting sentence. She dropped her feet to the floor and slid up into a seated position on the edge of the bed. The room was cool. She checked the light coming through the windows high on the wall. Early morning, she guessed. Ted wasn't in the apartment. She'd sense it if he was. She looked down at her arms. No blood. Strange that. She'd been covered with it. He must have cleaned her up.

Did he...?

That was always the risk of getting physical with him. Toady was such a creep. Who knew what might get him off? Her hands ran down her aching body and along her thighs. *No.* She dismissed it. It was a crazy notion. In the state he was in, he couldn't have. She checked the clock. It wasn't early morning. It was late the following day.

Damn him.

He'd shot her up. She went to the bathroom, unsteady on her feet, touching the wall to keep her balance.

India?

What was that all about? He was like a dog with a bone on that topic. Had she met him there? People came and went like ships in the night on the backpacking trail. So maybe. She closed the door behind her and sat on the stool by the vanity, remembering another positive. Cameras. He'd told the truth. No cameras in the bathroom. If he'd seen her making the shiv, she'd never have gotten to use it. That gave her a boost. This patch was hers. All she had to do was shut the bathroom door and her world would be hers alone. Her head clearing, she stood up in front of the mirror and inspected herself.

No sign of blood anywhere.

He'd cleaned her up good and—

Her hand shot up to her throat.

How did I miss it?

A necklace.

No, not a necklace. That was a delicate thing. This was bigger, bolder. A choker. She ran her hands over it.

Flowers, butterflies.

It was beautiful but unexpectedly heavy.

A gift?

That made no sense. She'd tried to kill him, or half-kill him, to be technically correct, and judging by the look and feel of it, this was a pricey accessory. She reached behind her neck, planning to remove it and take a shower. But the latch was tricky and she soon gave up. The important thing was to shower with or without the choker.

She stood naked under the rainfall showerhead, soaking up the heat of the water before switching to cold and letting the chill of it numb her aches and clear her head.

Dressed in a bathrobe, she returned to the bedroom, the flashy choker on her mind. She sat on the bed and toyed with it.

A control symbol?

His idea of a dog collar most likely. But he'd soon learn she was not a dog and nobody's slave, either.

"Hi, Cass." His voice boomed and his face lit up the TV.

A dramatic entrance.

And one she wanted to ignore, but for once, his face was a joy to look at. His left cheek sported a wad of gauze tied down with an adhesive bandage. That almost got a smile out of her.

The wine glass.

Nice shot.

The moment done, she turned away, sitting on the side of the bed, staring at the empty wall.

"You're still angry. Okay, I get it. I was hoping you'd calmed down. That was quite a shot I gave you. No choice about that. I needed stitches at the hospital. I told them I'd had a gardening accident, falling on a hedge trimmer. I don't think they believed me. They asked me why I was gardening at night."

Cass closed her eyes.

Looking at him without spitting hate was a simple task on the face of it, but it loomed in front of her like an insurmountable peak. She took a long breath and held it, wrestling with the simmering cauldron inside her. She had to engage with him or she'd never get the story on this choker. She blew it out, hoping her black mist anger would hitch a ride on the *whoosh.*

Get a grip! You're locked in a cage. Diving into a pit of denial or tuning into a fantasy world will not unlock the door.

What made it worse was how close she'd gotten. Close hurt so much more than abject failure. But it didn't change a damn thing. Close was a million miles away from success.

Stitches!

At least she had a consolation prize. Now she had to play it smart and keep up the pressure. She'd only have to succeed once. She opened her eyes and turned to look up at the screen, swiveling her body and pulling up a bent leg to rest it folded on the bed.

"Good. I hope it hurt."

"I understand you're upset. But what about me? You've got a few bruises. I lost pints of blood."

"But not enough."

"And they had to give me antibiotics. I could have died—"

"Boo-hoo."

"You wouldn't be laughing then. You'd starve to death. Better to bleed to death than starve, I'd say." He stopped and waited. But Cass left it there. She had plenty more bad simmering inside her, but she'd can that and save it for another day. "This has to be a turning point. In future, we need to—"

"What's this?" Cass reached up, her fingers on the choker.

"That's the future." He looked down and fiddled with his keyboard. "You know what they say… a picture is worth ten thousand words. So that would make a video worth… what? A million words." He finished with the keyboard and looked up. "In case you're wondering, chokers are coming back according to my fashion expert. I saw that one on the neck of that singer… what's her name? She looked gorgeous in it. But still not a patch on you. Cost me over eight hundred pounds. Anyway, here's the show."

Ted and the Caribbean backdrop disappeared and he reappeared outside in a field studded with shrubs. Behind him, a distant wall of trees and bushes looked like the start of a forest. Ted stood next to a table, empty except for a melon mounted on a base. It was standing up on end like the sculpted head of a Roman goddess. How odd, she might have thought if her eyes hadn't zoomed in on the choker draped around it. Yes, it was a dead ringer for the one on her neck.

"So anyway, I made a few modifications to the original choker."

Spider legs of fear crept up her spine, tingling at the back of her neck. So that explained the weight. Her fingers probed, finding something plasticky and lumpy on the inside.

"It's voice-activated like Siri. Of course, after that quick-thinking phone call you made, I don't need to explain to you how it works." He waved his hand at the melon like the host on a shopping channel selling a budget kitchen appliance. "My voice only, though." He chuckled. "Anyway, this one"—he touched the melon—"is called Melbot, and your one"—he nodded towards her—"is called Cassbot." He shrugged. "Not very original, I know." He was so enjoying himself, and his joy was a stick poking deep into her craw. "Melbot, activate." A red butterfly ornamenting the melon's choker flashed on and off. "Now let's say the melon misbehaves. For example, if I asked the melon a question politely in a civil manner, and it turned its back on me, refusing to answer. Now that's not nice." He crossed his arms over his chest, staring into the camera, eyeballing her virtually. She got the idea he'd rehearsed this over and over. "Melbot choke!"

Cass's hands slid down from her throat and her jaw dropped in slow motion. The choker tightened on the melon, driven by a high-pitched whine. Tighter and tighter, until juice flowed, its thick skin burst, and pulp dribbled down onto the table.

"It's perfectly calibrated." He chuckled again. "I hope. The Cassbot, I mean. It shouldn't draw blood on the choke command. But right about now, you'd find breathing pretty awkward and oxygen a bit scarce in the old noggin." He tapped his head with his knuckles. "You probably have some questions at this point. For example, you're probably wondering, what if the melon gets extremely naughty, not just rude, but downright naughty? Let's say the melon was to make me very angry by hacking away at my thigh with a china knife until my blood squirted all over the place. Well, here's your answer." He turned to the melon. "Melbot kill."

She didn't want to watch, to give him that pleasure. But not wanting was a dam soon breached, and one by one her tears rolled, her face motionless, her eyes on the screen. That high-pitched whine was now a banshee howl. It cut through her as surely as it did the melon. Pulp smashed and juice dribbled until the top half of the melon rolled onto the table and the choker stopped, its work done. Ted scooped up the pulp with his fingers and fed it into his mouth. "Yummy... Honey Bun cantaloupe, they call this." He twirled his finger around its mashed golden flesh. "Just about the same size as your neck."

The video ended and Ted was back on the Caribbean beach. He was holding the Melbot choker, now cleaned up since its field trip. He held it up admiringly. "Had it made in China. My design. Took them eight months. Got a special steel company to make the cutting cable. Super light, but super strong. Titanium and aluminum, plus some other exotic metals. Eight hundred pounds was only the cost of the choker itself, the electronics and the motor etcetera cost me over ten times that." He smiled, treacle sweet. Then he put the choker down and out of sight. When he looked back at the camera, his sickly smile was gone, replaced with phony sincerity.

Cass wiped the wet from her face with a brusque sweep of her knuckles. She wasn't broken and this was not going to break her. She'd find a way.

"But I'm worth it. Isn't that what you're trying to say?"

Whatever he'd had on the tip of his tongue, he swallowed it and stared. Evidently, defiance with a sniff of humor was not what he'd been expecting.

"I meant it... *Honey Bun*. This is our turning point. You might see it as a prison chain. But it's the opposite. That choker is tuned to sensors at the perimeter of the property. If you ever cross them, the kill command will trigger automatically. Same thing if you try breaking it with bolt cutters. So now I can give you more freedom. I don't have to keep you locked up in the apartment. You can even go out into the grounds. It's beautiful outside at this time of year. So long as you don't go out the front gate or over the fence. That'd be too far. I did this demo, so you'd be very clear. The last thing I want to do is search the grounds for your head."

"I wish I had killed you. I'd rather take my chances with starvation than this."

"You think that now because you're angry, but you'll get used to it. It's a lovely house and a huge estate. As soon as you calm down, you can have the run of it. I didn't want to do this. If you'd treated me like a human being and understood all I wanted was to get to know you, you wouldn't be wearing it. But this..." He waved down at his thigh. "Stitches. Blood. It has to stop. That choker is our wedding ring. You belong to me or nobody."

"I'll take nobody. I've never belonged to anyone and I never will."

"What if I let you go? What then? You fix everything with Rob Washington and live happily ever after. You're not dumb enough to believe that."

This was bait, and even though she could see the hook, she went for it.

"It happens. One partner cheats, but life goes on. That's what grown-ups do. In the real world, princesses don't fall in love with slimy toads that kidnap them."

Her razor-sharp barbs sounded good to her, but they bounced off him, his grin not registering as much as a twitch.

"How's it going to work, you and Rob? You share a jail cell?"

"I already know about the detective. That's nothing. Some compliance thing. No one goes to jail for that."

She waited while he keyed in a few strokes at the computer, still with the grin.

"No video this time. But you'll recognize the voices."

Indeed, she did, and however much she wanted to run and hide, she had to listen.

"I don't have much time." Pix, her voice a whisper with a sharp edge.

"Where are you?" Rob picked up on it.

"In the ladies. At the office. They're here again."

"The cops?"

"They have a warrant. A whole team of them. The screwdriver brigade."

"The what?"

"IT cops. Forensics. I don't know. They're taking office computers."

"They can't do that. Did you check the warrant?"

"Of course, I bloody didn't. You think I'm a lawyer. I called Jamie. It's for real." Cass had met Jamie socially. He was the company's solicitor, their lawyer, handily located in the same building two floors down. "They were grilling me. They kept asking about your laptop."

"Don't worry. It's here with me in the apartment."

A toilet flush brought the conversation unceremoniously to a close.

"So what," Cass said. "They're on a fishing expedition."

"Sure they are. And if they get that laptop, they'll land a monster."

"How do you know?"

"Because I've been there—his laptop—want to join me on a tour?" Cass said nothing. He'd hacked Rob's phone. He'd already proven that. So why not his laptop? "I've been in it for two years."

He let that sit with her before going on.

Was there a secret message in that two-year remark? Yes, that was when she'd seen him. She couldn't pin the date down exactly, but it was way back when she'd started with Rob.

Ted worked the keyboard some more and an image flashed up on the screen, a document. "Recognize it?"

She studied it but made no reply. It was a power of attorney for BlockTrend Analytics Inc, a company registered in the British Virgin Islands. What could she say? She'd never seen that document in her life, and yet there it was, appointing her as the company's attorney with pages of legalese that boiled down to one thing. She controlled the company, including its bank accounts.

Ted scrolled on to the last page, clearly enjoying himself. "Apostille. See all the stamps. That means they had it witnessed in front of a judge. That makes it valid anywhere on the planet."

"But I wasn't there. How could they—"

"No need. He'd got your name, address, and passport. All he had to do was fake your signature and pass it all to his lawyer. No worries. The lawyer probably went to school with the judge. It's an old boy network." Her head was spinning. She so wanted to disbelieve it, to challenge its existence. But a creeping feeling told her otherwise. She waited, not confrontational now, wanting more, and Ted was happy to oblige. "Know what fraud is?"

"Stealing money with a pen instead of a gun."

"More or less. And it requires a special skill set, stuff your ex is very good at—lying, cheating, stealing."

"What does this company do?"

"Deception. That's its real business. Supposedly, it was set up to research new crypto coins and business opportunities."

"But what does it really do?"

"Stuff money into Washington's pocket."

"Money from where?"

"CoinAxis, his company. He's funneling—he'd say investing—customer funds from CoinAxis into BlockTrend Analytics, a promising new growth company in the crypto sector."

"But they must produce something."

"Sure they do. He's got a team of high school kids in Vietnam who kick out crypto reports they work up with AI. So long as there's plenty of buzzwords in them, he calls it progress. Meanwhile, BlockTrend, or rather you, pay for this so-called research to companies that Washington owns for real."

"How much?"

"Half a billion and change."

Cass wanted to challenge that and tell him he'd gone too far with this nonsense. But the proof was already scrolling up on the screen. Bank statements for an account that she controlled. $20-$30 million a month. The volume of money and the implications of her connection to it left her shocked and shaky.

"It can't be that easy, diverting money like that. It's obviously—"

"Fraud. You're right. But then again, is it? Rob Washington is not a director or shareholder in BlockTrend Analytics. It's an unrelated company. He's stuffed the board with nominees, lawyers and the like. Legally, he doesn't run it either. You do. He owns the companies at the end of the money trail. But he's put a firebreak between CoinAxis and them. Its name is Cass."

"Shit…"

"Didn't you ever wonder why your wedding bells kept getting kicked down the road? Some of that was Pix. And this was the rest. If he marries you, his house of cards gets even more shaky. Easy to get you both on a conspiracy charge if you're husband and wife. But now, if he dumps you and sails off into the sunset with Pix, he'll live happily ever after. You're the perfect patsy, into it neck deep without even knowing it exists. Either way, if the cops get that laptop, there's enough in it to put you both in jail."

Cass was struggling to keep up. Forensic accounting was not her strong suit. But she'd gotten the gist of it. Rob had fucked her over. He'd have a plausible excuse for dropping her in this dung heap—he always had one of those—and a credible explanation as to why it was the best thing that had ever happened to her. But setting that aside, she…

Her rambling thoughts hit a wall.

"You tipped off the FBI. You started this whole damn thing. It was you." The realization kicked open a floodgate of memories, and that elusive moment, the anonymous face at the office she could never remember, flashed before her eyes. As part of the ad agency team working on the CoinAxis account, she'd been at their offices during a ransomware attack. Hackers had locked up the company's network and threatened to zap all their data unless they paid up. They told her everything was under control. They'd hired a specialist, a world-class encryption expert, to clean up the mess. She was making a presentation when she saw him. He was in the data room across the corridor dwarfed by racks of computers. But he wasn't working at a keyboard. He was standing at its glass wall, staring at her as though he was witnessing his first sunrise. Filling in the gaps from there was easy. To do his job, he'd have needed administrator credentials, all their security keys and passwords. With that in his pocket, hacking his way into Rob's world must have been child's play. "You did it. You bastard."

"Oh... I almost forgot. Silly me. Cassbot, activate."

A faint click and a momentary throb at her throat and it was done.

She touched the choker, a reflex. Then her hands dropped to her sides. She didn't want to put on a show for him, give him the pleasure of seeing her suffer. But that was a faint hope. The injustice of it all hit her like a spike. Not just the choker, but the whole of it, abducting her, torturing her with her cheating-man's sex tape, and now this, triggering a legal nightmare that could have her wake up in jail. Anger surged up in her chest, anger going nowhere, drowned in helplessness. Desperation squeezed a burst of tears out of her. She rubbed them away with a clenched fist.

No... you don't get that. You don't get to see my hurt.

But he already had.

"Hey..." The paper show scrolling on-screen vanished. "Don't cry." His massive face filled the screen. He had to be close enough to the camera to kiss it. She could see every pore on his nose, every glint of sweat.

"I'm not crying. I leaked an emotion is all. They come and go and that one's gone."

He was close all right, close enough to read his face like a book, the lines riddling his forehead, the regret in his watery blue eyes.

"Don't be sad. This is freedom day. I can unlock the apartment now. We can walk in the grounds. It's a lovely day." He waited, but she said nothing with her mouth and even less with her eyes. His frown deepened. "Did you see the antipasti I left you? Check the dining room. It's all your favorites. I ordered it in from that Italian place. When you freshen up, get something to eat and get dressed. It's sunny, but there was a shower last night. The ground's a little soft. But you won't need wellies. Put on something comfortable for walking. Those Cloud 5 sneakers would be ideal. I read about them in Harper's Bazaar. They're waterproof, so a patch of wet grass won't trouble you. I can show you the house too and the gardens. I've been wilding one of the meadows. I saw a Blue Adonis yesterday. That's a butterfly. It was gorgeous, feeding on a bird's-foot flower. I planted a bunch of those last year. That's gourmet stuff to them."

He waited some more, but Cass was still in listening mode and liking what she was hearing. No, it wasn't the promise of fresh air and sunshine lifting her spirits, but the birth of hope. Ted was a monster, but a very human monster. Anger bounced off him. But look what a few tears had done.

10

Ted poured a glass of milk and sat at the kitchen table. He needed a moment to catch up.

With what? With himself.

He'd fast-forwarded the plan.

A summer's day walk in the garden had always been a part of it, something to cherish when she had accepted her fate. But it was about to happen twenty-four hours after she'd attacked him with lethal weapons. He'd changed the plan on a whim, and that didn't fit his check-the-box world. He took his milk upstairs to his bedroom and lay on the bed. The wall TV was still tuned in to the CCTV in the apartment, but there was no sign of Cass. She'd be in the bathroom or in front of the dressing room mirror fiddling with the choker, trying to figure out how to get it off without killing herself. His thoughts moved on to Washington's laptop, his stash of naughty secrets. The police needed it to make their case. Seizing something like that meant an arrest warrant couldn't be far behind. Ted logged in to Cyclops from his phone to spy on Washington.

The big man was on the move, his phone picking up the clickety-click of a London taxi, a black cab, and not one of the new electric types but an old-school diesel. The journey went on and on with voices in the background too muffled to make sense of, chitchat with the driver getting picked up by the phone in his pocket. Uber was Washington's usual ride of choice. But here he was in a black cab. Most likely he'd hailed it on the street. Had he done that on purpose to avoid a digital trail? Was he that paranoid already? Ted checked his geolocation. He was on his way to Monty's place in Kew. Had to be. His guess was confirmed minutes later when Washington made the call to announce his arrival.

"Hey, Monty. Okay if I stay tonight?"

"Sure. You know that. What's up ... fight with Pix?"

"I wish..." Ted sat up, eager to get the rest of this. "I'll tell you later. I'm in a taxi. Any news on that van's registration plate?"

"You're not going to like it. The plates were registered to a Toyota, not a Mercedes van. They were nicked off the car a few weeks back. I told you they'd be stolen. No one is going to put a fake sign on a van, then use real plates."

Washington hung up after greeting that news with a few expletives, and Ted followed his journey, his eyes dancing from the taxi's beacon on the London street map on his phone to the CCTV on the wall screen. Cass had emerged from the bathroom wearing a robe and she was going about her business in a relaxed and orderly fashion.

Relaxed and orderly.

That didn't help the anxiety rumbling in his belly. Her attack had been preceded by an eerie calm like this. But surely the choker would make her think twice about going down that road again. He didn't plan to carry a weapon anymore. He had his voice after all. If she strayed, he'd have her on her knees within seconds. What a eureka moment that had been—the day he'd invented the choker. He'd been watching the entertainment news and there'd been this singer, Dua what's-her-name, on the red carpet at a movie premiere in Leicester Square. She'd looked gorgeous in a stunning dress. But what had caught his attention even more was her choker. Pastel colors. Flowers and butterflies. The TV cameras had zoomed in on her. Gleaming-teeth smile. Jet black hair. Swish-swish. The paps went crazy. Click-click, flash-flash. And just like those flashing bulbs, the idea had come to him. Buy that choker and fit it on the inside with a voice-activated restraint. The beta model had used an electric shock like those special collars for bad dogs. But Cass was not a dog. Besides, a few volts of pain wasn't enough. Cass was too willful. She had to know her living or dying was down to him. And what a product he'd built. He'd even fantasized about selling it on the dark web. The ad copy would write itself...

Wife getting out of line? Got a girlfriend who's not trying hard enough? Problem solved. Buy her a **Yoker***. Our patented fashion choker is every woman's must-have accessory, guaranteed to perfect every man's love life and ensure conjugal bliss.*

Yes, he'd had a few chuckles about that idea.

More seriously, she'd behave now. She'd do what she was told. That was all he'd ever wanted. She'd be the person he needed her to be. Too bad it had come to this. It was such a brutal piece of kit. Ted wasn't even sure if he could do it.

Could I choke her?

It took him a moment, but the answer was yes.

Could I kill her?

Some people thought killing butterflies was gruesome. But other people went around the country strangling human beings. To serial killers, that was normal. Maybe it made them feel complete, like collecting butterflies for him. He dropped that line of thinking. It was absurd anyway. It would never come to that.

The taxi's location beacon stopped moving.

Monty's place in Kew.

Ted swept aside his philosophical rambling and tuned back in to Washington's phone, adjusting the audio as Washington settled in his usual spot on the couch in Monty's lounge. Ted could see none of this except in his head, the camera being in Washington's pocket until he set it on the table, aimed at those ugly light fittings on the ceiling. That was all Ted could see apart from a brown paper bag standing upright next to the phone. He listened. But there was still no talk. Just beer cans—their rings getting pulled—and the shuffling of one of them prepping a smoke. Not a word passed between them. No handshakes, no hugs, no hellos. That was how best mates did it. No talk, not necessary. They'd been buddies since college, and blood brothers since Washington had lied to the cops to keep Monty out of jail. Totally comfortable, one with the other, they'd have made a perfect couple if only they were gay.

Ted couldn't help it, but the more he thought about them, the more he felt it—envy. He'd tried making friends. But trying had a battery and it had run out. In his preteens, he'd figured out why. After he'd popped out of the womb—whosever womb it was, she hadn't hung around long enough for him to find out—a nurse had dunked him in people repellent. So that was that. A bestie like Monty was something he could only dream of. But that was okay. He could live with it. He had Cass, the ultimate woman, the gigastacy of every man's dreams.

"Cops turned up at the office this morning. They took a few computers. They had a warrant." Washington finally broke the silence with today's headline news, piquing Ted's curiosity even more. What was he doing on Monty's couch in Kew? After that frantic phone call from his lover this morning, why wasn't he in her cozy nest soothing her frazzled nerves? Sure, these two guys were best mates, coming across like psychoanalysts swapping freebie sessions in some of their conversations. But not on a night like this.

More beer gulping and burps.

"Hold on… I'm not following this. The cops showed up at your office with a warrant. So you visited your mate who has two kilos of weed and 500 grams of uncut Peruvian in his basement."

"The warrant wasn't for me. It was for the computers."

"Even so…"

"I had no choice. I was at Pix's. We were about to have dinner—"

"Tonight?"

"That's what I'm telling you. And I popped out to grab some wine. Here"—Washington's hand reached into the camera frame and pulled a bottle out of the brown paper bag—"be my guest."

"Rob, what the—"

"I'm getting there. Luckily, I went to that place on Portobello Road instead of the corner shop. I wanted to get something special. Calm her down. The walk took me half an hour and when I got back, the cops were there at the flat. Two cars. One unmarked, the other a patrol car. They were after my laptop."

"Which is where?" There was no audible answer. But Ted filled in the blank with the obvious, Washington's dour face and dejected shrug. "So now they've got your laptop. Containing what?"

"Kryptonite … if they can get through the encryption. But that'll take them months."

"No, it won't. They'll arrest you and get a court order compelling you to give them the password. If you refuse, you'll go to jail anyway." Ted didn't know if that was true or not, but as a purveyor of mindbending substances to the crypto crowd, Monty probably had the inside track on what police could and couldn't do.

Washington is on his way to jail.

That was a happy thought. But Ted felt the first tremors of something else. Not sure what, but he was not happy.

There was a long pause. Even listening in, Ted could sense the tension. This was his private radio play, a thriller with the suspense building until Monty burst the bubble. "What the hell happened to you?"

Wow... where did that come from?

Ted had lost the plot. He leaned in closer to the speakers. There was a new tone in Monty's voice. Disappointment, disgust? It was one of the two or someplace in the middle.

"What?"

"You used to be such a straight-up guy. Now Cass gets taken and you abandon her."

"It's not like that."

"You're shacked up with your girlfriend. What's that? And then—when the cops show up there—you hightail it over to your best mate, the drug dealer. Do the words collateral damage mean anything to you?"

"Can I stay or not?"

"You know the answer." Monty's hand took hold of the wine and it disappeared from view. "Might as well drink this stuff."

"I'll order the pizza." The posh candelabra vanished, turning into blackness as Washington's big hand picked up the phone.

Ted left the conversation there. No interest in their pizza order. As for their conversation from this point on, while entertaining from the voyeuristic point of view, it would yield nothing of value to him. The interlude had bucked him up. Washington's trip from hero to zero was almost complete. He'd lost his fiancée, was close to losing his lover, and his best friend was about to dump him. How could he use this information to help him maneuver Cass? The noose was tightening on Washington more quickly than he'd expected. He could relay the news to her, but why? There was no obvious advantage in doing so, and it might backfire.

What if it triggered sympathy?

My poor Rob needs me.

That was a risk. Better to wait. Washington's world was disintegrating. He'd have to do something major, run away to some distant land and take his girlfriend with him. That would be superb. He'd break that news to Cass within seconds. But what if Monty's preaching won the day? What if he grew a conscience and went to the police? There'd be a major manhunt and she'd have every reason to hope.

Cass had disappeared into her dressing room. Was she getting ready for the grand tour? She hadn't said yes. But she hadn't said no either, and she was getting ready for something.

He went into his bathroom and checked himself in the mirror, probing the dressing on his cheek with a gentle finger. There was no blood seeping through, and the painkillers had dulled the pain throughout his body. He double-checked his thigh. All good. No blood. His jeans were tight around his thigh, so the bulge of the dressing they'd put on the wound was visible. He thought about changing them for a baggier pair but decided against it. Advertising the wound might earn him a few sympathy points and remind her of what she'd put him through. He stared at his reflection and worked on his state of mind, running through a self-help mantra to get pumped and positive.

We had a row. But that's history.

As the great man once said—Time starts now.

And so, with Steve McQueen's line from *Bullit* still echoing in his head, he headed downstairs.

11

Cass stood at the threshold, relishing a moment of disbelief.

It's open.

That steel-lined door behind the curtain, it was open. She peered through to the dimly lit basement beyond, oddly fearful.

Why?

It didn't make sense. Prisoners ran when the gate fell open. Yet here she was, taking her time, considering the next step as though it might be a long one. Some sort of hostage syndrome thing. She didn't know what. In just a few days, she'd grown into it, her cave, her comfort. This was her apartment now, the beyond, unknown.

She swept aside this cold draft of madness with a shudder and pressed on out into the basement. A dim light came from a cracked door to one side. She peeked through. Computers, racks of them, and shelves piled high with tech this and tech that. She edged a half step closer. Could there be an old cell phone hidden in any of that? Just the thought put a bolt of excitement through her. But she stepped back. No chance. Ted had plenty of human weaknesses, but stupidity, carelessness and oversight were not among them. He was as calculating as a robot. She took in the rest of the basement with a glance, a wine rack that slid back and forth concealing the door, barrels and boxes. With the wine rack back in place, this would be what it once was, a wine cellar and perfect camouflage for a clandestine penitentiary.

A line of LEDs marked out a ramp and a stairway heading up. She took the ramp, pushed open the unlocked door at the top and stepped out into a reception hall where she stopped, listening. She was standing under a flight of creaky wooden stairs. She knew they were creaky because they creaked under Ted's feet. Yes, he was right above her, a spring in his heels as he bounced down the steps. Heading off across the hall, he caught sight of her lurking under the stairs and jerked back with a grunt.

"I found my own way out," she said, mustering a smile. "Thanks for leaving the door open." That seemed to do the trick, and he relaxed but was still lost for words. "Are you going to show me around?"

He nodded.

"Although I should warn you, with your design background, some of it's going to be pretty painful."

Cass had figured as much already. The house, or what she could see of it, was not a continuation of the apartment. It couldn't have been more different. Her eyes took it in with a single sweep. The centerpiece of the hall was a round wooden table on a single leg, empty save for a bronze casting of an unimaginably ugly horse head.

"Who would have thought you could fit so much old wood into one room?" That was as kind of a comment as she could make. The walls, the floor, the stairs—all wood. Add to that the twisty wooden beams above them and that left just a few patches of white in a world of brown and black.

"Yeah... not guilty. It was like this when I bought it. Been in one family for a few hundred years."

"And they never spent a dime on it." She pointed at a dressmaker's dummy tucked in one corner. It was dressed in a satin jockey's jacket in lime green and orange. "Horse lovers?"

"With no taste. Even I can see that. But I made one small upgrade. Let me show you something beautiful before we go outside." He led her through an open doorway into... "The estate agent called this the drawing room. That's what posh people called a living room back then. Nothing to do with drawing though, so don't get excited. She told me it was short for withdrawing room. People used to withdraw from—"

"Riding ugly horses?"

He laughed, all toothy grin and staccato breath. He loved that, their first conversation that wasn't a fight. It was that easy.

"That and whatever. Then they'd relax in here." They stopped and looked around. Plenty of wood here too and lots of exposed red bricks. "My aunt would have called it a parlor." His face fell, and that grin went with it.

"Are you close to her?" Cass sensed a pressure point. He'd never mentioned his family before.

"She was my guardian. Court-appointed. Anyway"—he waved his hand, getting back on topic—"I call it a living room. I didn't change anything here either. Nothing except the fish photos."

"Fish?"

"People with big smiles holding dead fish. I gave them all to a charity shop. They were happy to get them, said they'd sell them easy. That makes no sense to me. Why would anyone buy a photo of a man holding a dead fish?"

"Okay... so the beautiful thing I'm about to see is not a fish. I figured out that much."

"It's over here." He led her to the room's only stretch of white wall where they stood in front of two framed photos. "Here he is, the Kaiser, the Emperor of India. And here she is." He pointed to the smaller of the two butterflies. "His wife, the Empress." They were both green with black-trimmed wings and white dots, but the male was so much more glorious. Even splayed under glass in this creaky old farmhouse, he looked full of life as though he could break out of his glass tomb and fly away at any moment.

"Beats dead fish. I'll give you that. And what's this one?"

It wasn't a butterfly but a photo of a much younger Ted receiving a trophy. She peered closer at it. A butterfly in Perspex.

"Photography award. And there's the photo that earned me it. That's my High Brown Fritillary."

"How do they come up with these names?"

Ted stared at the photo as if lost in the moment he'd captured it.

"I took that shot just up the road." Next to the photo was a framed edition of the American Butterflies magazine with Ted's photo on the cover. "It took me months of waiting. But I got it."

"You sure did." He was getting that creepy, obsessed look in his eyes. "How about we get some fresh air and look for some live butterflies?"

"Great idea." He snapped out of it, his eyes lighting up and his pallid cheeks flushing red at the prospect.

They walked across the hall and into a long, narrow kitchen. Quite a shock this one. In contrast to the ugliness of the hallway with its wooden floorboards and ugly horse shrine. This was a room to live in, warm and cozy, welcoming almost. Any prisoner fresh out of their cell would have noticed and with her artist's eye that went double for Cass. She scooped up details as they made their way to the back door. The time-worn flagstone floor and oak-framed ceiling had to be hundreds of years old, but they were balanced with modern stainless steel appliances set in eggshell blue cabinetry and topped with polished granite. Whoever had designed her sublime apartment had been set loose here too.

They passed through a rustic wooden door into sunlight and Cass breathed it all in. Yes, she had a plan going on in the back of her head, and yes, she was looking for something, anything, a trigger to shoot the starting pistol of her escape. But she needed a break too. She needed to breathe. She needed a moment to recover and recharge. Design-perfect, it might be, but her apartment was still a jail. Here was the natural world dialed up to maximum, all of her senses shooting vials of it into her brain. They walked out onto a neatly trimmed lawn, Ted leading the way at first, then dropping back so they were walking side-by-side. Cass spun her head, taking it all in, the red brick façade of the house behind them, the sunlit glow of the green-gold world beyond it, and the earthy fragrance of soil mixed with the scent of freshly mown grass.

Leaving the curated area around the house, they crossed open fields dotted with wildflowers. Cass had a script ready and a performance to give, but she couldn't bring herself to hit the play button. Not yet. They had time. And for the moment, Ted seemed happy to walk in a silence she was delighted to share, a silence broken only by the hum of bees foraging in flowers and the caw of rooks circling above. They headed towards a pond in the distance. That was what he called it—the pond. But it was hard to tell what it was from this distance. It could even have been a river or a lake. What she couldn't see were fences marking the perimeter where the choker's sensors were located. Most likely, they were hidden by the trees and bushes that ringed the fields. Ted owned an impressive stretch of country, and operated as a business, it would have made a good-sized pasture farm running cattle, horses or sheep. But here it was, left to grow wild by a butterfly lover. As they approached the pond, Cass pointed to a tiny blue butterfly dancing around a yellow flower.

"Is that one rare?"

Ted laughed. "If I tell you it's called a Common Blue, you can probably guess."

"What got you started on this?"

"Butterflies?"

"Math prodigy, computer games, butterflies? It's a weird fit."

His smile, and the moment he took to compose an answer, told her how much her interest meant to him.

"My aunt Nell started me off on it."

"The posh one?"

"Yeah... in her own mind anyway." There it was again, that landside of a face.

"So it runs in the family?"

"No, she hated butterflies, especially when they were babies."

"Caterpillars?"

"She said I spent too much time at the computer. So she made me work in the garden with her, made me her slave. She had me digging up potatoes and pulling cabbages. So one day, she holds up a caterpillar, wriggling between her stubby fingers right in front of my eyes. I was only eight or nine. Then she squelched it and wiped her hands on her apron. Its head got stuck there, still twirling around a bit like *where's my body*? She made me squelch them too. There were a lot of Cabbage Whites that summer and she got a net to catch them. But she was too slow. So she gave it to me. Whenever I caught one, she'd rub it to nothing between her hands. I had to catch six every morning before lunch, or I'd go hungry."

"She sounds awful." Cass was laying it on thick here. Killing a few garden pests to save your cabbages didn't sound like a childhood trauma to her. But there he was, face twisted into a grimace like the smell of cow dung had just wafted in from a neighboring farm. He turned back towards the path and they carried on walking towards the pond.

"Anyway…" Ted said when he'd found his way back into the conversation. "I used to give her a few whites. There were always plenty of them. But now and again I'd catch something special, a Red Admiral or a Painted Lady. No way was I giving her a beautiful creature like that. So I kept a jar at the edge of the garden. I made holes in the top so the butterflies could breathe. I'd pop them in there. And later, I'd let them go. It was like a game in the end. Aunt Nell was the evil witch and I was the butterflies' champion. Like Superman is for humanity. But sometimes they'd die in my jar. I buried them at first. But then I learned I could keep them, and their beauty would live forever."

They reached a footbridge crossing an arm of the pond and Cass grabbed the rail instinctively as they walked over it, the weathered planks creaking under her feet. "Don't worry," Ted said. "Back when it was a farm, cows used to walk over this, the smart ones anyway. Save them from walking around the pond." They stopped halfway across and leaned on the railing, enjoying the view of a twisty body of water edged by reed beds and shaded by mature trees.

"Where's John Constable now we need him?"

"Constable?" The sudden alarm on Ted's face confused her. Then it came to her.

"Oh, that's funny." She put her hands up to cover her mouth. Laughing to his face wouldn't help her cause. "He was a famous English landscape artist." She waved her hand at the scene. "He'd have loved this spot."

"I thought you said—"

"Police constable. Yeah, I get it. We don't use that word."

Ted looked back at the pond and its surrounds.

"You should paint it. I could get you paints and things."

"Maybe… is that mean aunt your only family?" Cass looped back into their earlier conversation, fishing for information. The more she knew about him, the easier it would be to navigate her way through the maze of his brain.

"Was. And I wouldn't call her family."

There it was again, the hurt face. Best to shut down that line of questioning. No point in backing him into a corner.

Not yet.

"So sad about your brother."

That caught her off guard. Was he fishing too? No, he knew where he was going, and now she did too.

India.

He was dropping breadcrumbs again, leading her back to where they'd first met. *Not for the first time*, he'd said, when she'd remembered seeing him in the office during the ransomware attack. At last, she had the answer to that mystery and the reason he'd mentioned India repeatedly. Maybe seeing him in the daylight had helped jog her memory too. He'd been so different back then.

"The Vivek Express. You were that Brit guy sitting opposite us with—"

"A beard and long hair… trying to fit in, look cool. Didn't work with you girls, though, did it?"

The answer was no, but the picture wasn't clear in her head. The truth was she barely remembered him. She'd spent a year backpacking in Asia. How many guys had hit on her? How many women too? Train stations, buses, hotel lobbies, beaches and bars.

Always with a casual opener and the sharp edge of hidden intent lurking behind their eyes. Reaching back, all she got was a shaggy Brit whose travels had kept him well clear of a shower for way too long, and definitely not one she wanted to take home to bed with her.

"So you remembered me when you saw me in the office?" He nodded. "Do you remember the other girl?" Cass had been traveling north, hoping to get in and out of Afghanistan. No good reason for that, or at least none that made sense to anyone but her. Her brother's remains had ended up back in the States with the Stars and Stripes draped over them. But seeing where it had happened had meant so much to her. The train ride had taken days, but it had felt like months, and she'd struck up a friendship with another lone female traveler.

"I remember you both... how you met and became instant friends. Two Americans in a strange land. Superfast bonding. It's normal. Then it turned out you were both into art. Yackety-yak." He mimed a chatterbox with his hand. "I tuned out about there."

"That's all you remember?" Cass looked away as she spoke, her eyes drifting down to the fish feeding under the bridge, her fingers digging into the worn, grainy wood of the rail.

He didn't answer at first. Was he trying to remember? Or figuring out the best lie? Wait... Ted didn't lie. Like hell. Everyone lied when it suited them.

"I remember how you told me where to get off when I tried to make friends. If that's what you mean." Cass waited. She wanted the whole answer to this question. "Not much else. I dozed off a lot. I only remember about your brother because it upset you to talk about it. Did you ever make it to Helmand province?"

She shook her head, wishing she'd never brought up the subject of family. "By the time I got near the border, everything had gotten so bad. There was a Level 4 travel advisory—Do Not Travel—that's the US government saying *you're on your own, pal.* It was a crazy idea."

"Crazy, but beautiful. You'd loved him that much. And I didn't mind getting the brushoff. It made me sad, but I was used to it." He pulled himself off the railing and nodded towards the trail on the other side of the bridge. "Let's just enjoy today, shall we? This ancient history stuff is bringing me down."

She nodded. It was bringing her down too, with a thump. She followed him off the bridge and around the pond to a jetty where they sat and looked back towards the bridge. Cass probed the distance with her eyes, looking back the way they had come. Beyond the farmhouse were more fields and a driveway that snaked into invisibility, obscured by the rolling topography. Her line of sight ended at a wall of trees and bushes. She scanned them, finally making out a gate—a solid structure, head height, probably electric—setback between a gap in the trees.

The entrance, the way in—and her way out.

12

Ted unfolded one of his crossed legs with the help of his hands and stretched it out on the jetty. Mindful of the stitches in his thigh, he did it all slowly, like he was handling an unexploded bomb.

Cass nodded at the leg. "I'm sorry."

Her apology was so unexpected it left him fumbling for words. Finally, he said, "The painkillers help."

"I wasn't trying to kill you. I just wanted to wound you so badly you'd have to go to hospital. But it only made things worse in the end." She fingered the choker. "For both of us."

"There's something you should know. Why I made two chokers, both calibrated for your neck. It's because of the battery. Every two weeks I have to switch chokers to recharge the battery. It'll last much longer, but I need to do that as a precaution."

"Precaution?"

He looked around the pond, the trees, birds and butterflies, the dappled sunlight on the still water. What a shitty place to tell her. But he had to. There was no way around this. She had to know. It was for her own good and his. He shrugged at the landscape and turned to face her. She deserved the truth.

"If it gets too low—down to 25% or less—it triggers."

"It chokes me?"

He shook his head, averting his eyes when he saw the realization on her face, fear draining the color from her cheeks, leaving her pale and looking years older.

"Why don't we put it all behind us? The bad things I've done to you, and the bad things you've done to me. Believe me, I never wanted to put that thing on you."

She looked away, then down at the water. He gave her time, letting her process her new reality.

"It's pretty, at least," she said, putting a brave face on it.

"You can have more freedom now. Look…" He swept his arm, embracing the scene. "A lovely walk on a summer's day."

Cass fondled the choker.

"This got me thinking about everything. About all the effort you've put in. Not just creating this choker, but everything. The apartment, the security systems. I mean, how… how did it all happen? You had the idea to build this place, then find a girl to—"

"No, no." Ted jerked around, twisting so suddenly he had to catch his balance with one hand on the jetty. "It didn't start with the apartment or the choker. It started with you. All of this is for you—not *some girl*. You. Only you. It was the only way for us to be together."

"You saw me in India. Then you saw me a second time at the office, and you decided to—?"

"No, it was… do you believe in fate?"

"You mean… like karma?"

"That night, after I saw you in the office, I couldn't sleep, couldn't get you out of my head. So I sat up in bed and watched old movies, dozing on and off. And one time I woke up in the middle of a movie called *The Collector*. I couldn't believe it. The hero was a lepidopterist."

"A what?"

"A butterfly collector. It was a movie about a guy like me. Except he wasn't like me. He was a real loser, a nobody. He gets this unbelievable crush on Miranda. But she's out of his league. Different class. That was big back then. Class, I mean. Then he wins the lottery, and flush with money, he kidnaps her and keeps her in a special basement he's built. He thinks he's made it nice for her. But it's crap, dingy and unhealthy."

"So what happens?"

"She got sick. Of course she did. It was inhuman the way he was keeping her. She didn't even have her own bathroom."

"So she died?"

"Not from being sick, no."

"Then what?"

He frowned, hesitant, wondering why he'd even mentioned *The Collector*. This was not a story with a happy ending. At least, not for Miranda. "She kept trying to escape. So one day, when he was stopping her, he accidentally killed her."

Cass didn't respond at first, and he was about to change the subject when she said, "Did they have the death penalty here back then?"

"I think so."

"And they caught him?"

"Not exactly."

"So how did it turn out... exactly?"

"He buried her in the garden and moved on."

"Moved on to what?"

"A more suitable girl. Someone in his own class. Like the shop assistant he'd seen at Woolworths."

"And that's how it ends?"

He nodded. "With him watching the new girl, planning it, learning from his mistakes."

"What a horrible movie!"

"It was the 60s. They didn't do happy ever after back then."

"So that was your inspiration?"

"You were my inspiration. The movie was a guide showing me all the mistakes I had to avoid. Like windows. She had no windows. Daylight is important for good health. You've got windows, sort of...."

"Sort of?"

"When we were walking here, did you notice the basement windows from outside the house?" Cass shook her head. "It's a trick question. There are no basement windows. They're fake. Special lamps behind glass match the natural spectrum of daylight. Sensors outside the house monitor the intensity of natural light and match it." He grinned. Bragging rights were due. It had taken him weeks to program the algorithm and perfect the simulation. "You need daylight to synchronize your biorhythm. That basement is super healthy. Temperature, humidity, oxygenation, they're all perfect. No way were you going to get sick like Miranda. The Collector didn't have technology like that. He was in the Stone Age. Same with security. No locks and keys, no ropes."

"Just a collar that kills if you forget to change the battery. My... that's progress."

"I shouldn't have told you that. I shouldn't have even showed you that video. It was a mistake. I was angry."

"I don't get it. You do all this work and spend all this money. You say you love me, you'll do anything for me. But then this." Her hand went up to the choker. "Could you kill the person you love?" Ted writhed, but stuck on the jetty there was no dodging this one, no escape and no answer. Love. She'd said the word. She'd understood. But she'd wrapped it in a puzzle. "This is not love. It's control."

"It depends how you look at it."

"Everything does. But if you can kill me—if you are capable of that—you don't love me. You own me. You collected me and stuck me in a jar with holes punched in the lid to keep me healthy." Another silence followed. He was at a loss. Were these questions about love sincere, or was she playing a game? He loved playing video games, but not mind games, especially not with Cass. She was too good at them. "Do you love me?"

That didn't sound like a game, more like she wanted to know.

"Enough to spend two years of my life planning and building this. You're why I sold my company. You've been my full-time job ever since. The choker's not about love. It's about trust. I'd do anything for you, give you anything."

"Except freedom." He looked away from her, down at the water, the emptiness of the truth gnawing at him. "It's incredible technology. I'll give you that. Voice-activated. Bluetooth and Wi-Fi, I guess, linked to your phone." He nodded, watching them both in the mirrorlike surface of the pond. "Did you test it with other voices?" This conversation was going wrong. Ted sensed it and his eyes strayed from the couple in the wet mirror below the jetty to her face. He tried to read it but got nowhere. She was nodding slowly like a bobblehead dog in the window of a truck, a creepy smile transforming her face. "Could you give the command and see my blood spurt out into the pond?"

"It will never come to that. Why are you—"

"Let's kick the tires, run it around the block."

"What!"

"Cassbot"—her eyes locked on his, her voice booming—"kill." Panic ripped into him. But he quashed it in an instant. He'd tested the voice activation to the nth degree. She was wasting her time. The choker didn't even blink an LED. Even so, it had shocked him. She'd rolled the dice. She'd risked her life.

"Stop it!" He leaped to his feet, forgetting his injured thigh, and gasped at the sudden pain.

Cass was on her feet too, hunched forward, fists balled and white-knuckle tight. "Cassbot kill, Cassbot kill, Cassbot kill…"

He hollered at her to stop, but she wasn't listening.

What could he do? Trigger the choker? Say the words for her?

She'd kicked him out of the driver's seat once again and had both hands on the wheel. Her macabre chant hit him like hammer blows, her voice changing constantly, trying to match his vocal patterns. "Cassbot kill, Cassbot kill…" She'll never get there, he told himself. Then again, who knew? Against all odds, someone won the lottery every week. Ted stopped screaming. It didn't help. Besides, the algorithm might meld his voice with hers and…

He shook her. It shut her up momentarily. But as soon as he stopped, she started again, the chant getting closer and closer to mimicking his voice. He went to grab her, but as his hands jerked up, she slammed her fists into his chest, not punching but pushing, dropping low and putting all her weight into it. He'd been set up. The realization hit him as he hit the water and caught that final snapshot of Cass hightailing it off the jetty.

Bluetooth.

It came to him as he wriggled in the muddy slime at the bottom of the pond. How had he let that one slip past him? No Wi-Fi out here in the fields. And she'd know the limitations of Bluetooth, anyone with earbuds does. Twenty or thirty yards max. She was already out of range as he struggled to the surface and pulled himself up onto the jetty. She was out of voice range too. However hard he hollered, he'd never bring her to her knees with the choke command now. She was gone.

But why?

She'd never get beyond the perimeter.

He wiped the mud off his phone and broke into a trot. But lengthening his stride in the open field, he came to a sudden stop.

Of course...

She was running for the perimeter to force him to shut down the sensors. Outside the range of Bluetooth and with no Wi-Fi connection, he couldn't deactivate the choker. But he could dial into the security system and shut down the sensors. Her *Cassbot Kill* episode was another setup. She'd known what she was doing. He couldn't kill her. He'd admitted as much. He hadn't said the words, but she'd read it off his face. He set off after her and was soon running hard, and when he rounded the house, he saw her. She was halfway to the gate. That would burn up time. It was unclimbable, but the fence adjoining it wasn't, assuming she could get to it. For most of its length, it was lined with a jungle of bushes and trees. She'd have to work her way around to find an accessible stretch to climb. He knew where the gaps were. He could cut her off. It was that or shut down the sensors and let her escape. He stopped running and took out his phone. His fingers hovered over the keys, figuring the odds.

No. He put it away.

He'd leave the sensors up. He'd take the chance. Even if he got it wrong, she had to be bluffing. She'd never risk her life on his doing the right thing and shutting them down. Cass was at the gate, scouting her chances of scaling it. So he sprinted to a nearby stretch of fence fronted by sparse shrubbery. She'd end up there. He was sure of it. She was smart and it was the logical choice. He buried himself in bushes and waited. The fence was made of anti-scale, anti-cut, welded wire mesh, unclimbable according to its manufacturers. But he doubted that, and no way was he going to put it to the test. Even if it was unclimbable, there were plenty of trees nearby to give her a leg up.

He ducked down in the undergrowth, watching Cass approach and turn into the gap. She stood staring at the fence like she was calculating her options, body bent, hands on knees, belly heaving air through her open mouth. She was still too far away for him to tackle her. At this distance, a voice command might have worked, but he was reluctant to go that route. If it failed, she'd be gone, and this unscheduled cross-country run had made one thing clear—she was much fitter than him. He had to grab her before she had the chance to turn tail and run. She approached the fence, pausing between each step. Was she expecting a warning signal like the parking sensors on a car, an audible beep increasing in frequency as the sensors were approached? The thought alarmed him. The system had nothing like that, no audible alert. It was nothing, nothing, nothing—then you were dead. She'd think he'd turned off the sensors and go for it. She spun around on the spot. He guessed she was looking for trees with branches close to the fence. As she turned her back to him, he burst out of the shrubbery in a crackle of broken branches.

In an instant, Cass was off. She never even looked over her shoulder. She just blasted off like an Olympic sprinter. He dived and got lucky, his arm catching her trailing leg, and down she went. They slewed heavily into the grass, and he levered himself up on his toes and dived again. This time he had her, grabbing her leg as she kicked at him. He twisted her foot and rolled her onto her back, then threw himself on her. Yes, he had her, his body weight on top of her now, one hand covering her mouth and the other arm looped under her neck to stop her twisting her head away.

But suddenly, she stopped struggling, her body limp, no resistance, the only sounds his rasping breath and her heaving chest.

Her eyes were open, inches from his, their bodies pressed together.

She was waiting.

But for what?

He kept his hand on her mouth, afraid she'd start with that Cassbot mantra again, afraid too that this moment would end, this moment with their bodies fused into one, her heat triggering a warm glow in his belly. It would be so easy now to...

I could...

Or could I?

He eased his hand away from her mouth—just a tad—and she stayed silent. So he set it aside, resting his elbow on the floor, their eyes locked together, her heated breath on his face making him giddy.

Not like this.

He struggled, fighting it.

Fighting what?

Something inside him, something unthinkable.

He went to roll off of her but she grabbed him, her arm around his neck, her face jerking up to meet his. His mind blanked over, wiped clean by her lips tight against his, and her tongue deep in his mouth. He pushed her off, but she didn't let go, rolling him over and getting on top of him. "Fuck me, Ted. Do it." She kissed him again. Ted was on a funfair ride, everything happening too fast to track, too fast to breathe. She pinned him to the floor with one hand on his throat, her other hand sliding down his body and slipping under his belt.

No.

He snapped his head to the side to get his mouth free.

"No, please...."

"Fuck me. Right here. Fuck me, hard. Let's do it."

Too late.

Her hand was between his thighs. She had him, his softness. She squeezed and stroked. She had him. He tried to sit up, bunching his belly tight. But she used her bodyweight to push him back to the floor, one hand squeezing his throat, the other working his softness gently, tenderly...

His softness, his softness.

She stopped abruptly but didn't move her hands. He didn't react, a dull horror numbing his body. She withdrew both her hands, sliding them off him and sitting on the floor at his side.

"I get it... I get it now," she said.

"No, no... it's not what you think. I'm not like that. I've done it before. It's just that—"

"You poor sad bastard."

"No, no." He jumped to his feet and balled his fists, his face flushed, his eyes dancing from side to side but never catching hers.

"Let me go. You have to." She made a vague sweep with her arm. "I mean, what's the point? Where's this going? You never had a plan or even a dream. This was only ever a fantasy. Dreams can get real, fantasies never can. And if you keep me here, I'll kill myself. I don't need this collar and the sensors on the fence to do that. A broken glass will do. I'll find something. Sooner or later, I'll do it."

His mouth was half open, his jaw shifting this way and that, grinding out words they couldn't find. His eyes emptied, flushed blank with rage, and he banged his fists on his hips.

"Okay then... do it." He turned and strode off, then turned back. "Go ahead. Kill yourself. Climb the bloody fence. I'll collect your head in the morning."

Ted didn't look back. He wanted to. Oh boy, did he want to. But he'd never give her the pleasure of knowing he cared.

Back at the house, he ran up the stairs and locked himself in his bedroom. He sat on the bed and checked the CCTV system on his phone. There she was, walking back to the house, casually as though nothing had happened, as though she'd just finished a walk in the grounds. Anger and relief swirled in a mix, making him dizzy.

Bitch.

He'd leave her to her own devices. She could have the run of the house. She wouldn't chance the fence now. She'd tried to outfox him and failed. So she'd humiliated him out of spite, stuck him on a pedestal and nailed a plaque to it.

This is not a real man.

Well, she was wrong. He was a man. He could do it. He could...

The tape played on, running in a loop in his head. Night came and he dozed on and off. No sleep, no relief, only dreams he'd rather forget. He'd wake and see it again, their romp in the grass. He'd screw his eyes tight. But none of what had happened that day went away. It only replayed, over and over, its 3D intensity getting ever more real. Exhaustion finally claimed him and he fell asleep, waking hours later at dawn. Something had happened in the blackness of those hours.

A divine gift, an epiphany.

The answer had come to him, not as a dream, but as a realization the instant his eyes opened. He was going to set her free. The perfect solution. He had it.

13

Cass slept in the living room, stretched out on the long leather couch. It was a nice spot. Pushed up against a wall under leaded windowpanes, it ticked all her boxes, comfortable, well-lit, and—with a view back to the open doorway—secure. After that workout in the woods, she needed a shower and a change of clothes, but no way was she voluntarily returning to the basement, giving him the easy option of locking its door. If he wanted her back in there, he'd have to drag her kicking and screaming. She woke at dawn, and with no sign of Ted or sounds of movement, she headed for the guest toilet off the hall. It was primitive, just a WC, a sink and a mirror. She stared at the haggard face looking back at her. The mirror was faded at its corners, maybe not as old as the house but getting there. How many farmer's wives had stood in this spot and bemoaned the ravages of time and the toll they had taken on them?

How long has it been?

Four or five days before—or was it more?—she'd been Cassandra Beauvoir, the partner of crypto wunderkind, Rob Washington, and an incognito artist, hiding behind the alias Eden Matrix. Her, or rather his, augmented reality murals had won first prize at the prestigious Ars Electronica Festival. Now she was this... a farm girl, her face scrubbed and wan, her hair knotted in clumps like a bundle of straw.

Fuck it.

Why was she even thinking this?

Get your priorities straight.

She shook herself out of it, splashed her face with cold water, then cleaned up as best she could, flushing that worn, defeated look down the sink and pumping up her game face.

Feeling marginally better, she sat at the kitchen table and pondered her situation while the coffee brewed. She took the cup into the lounge and sat back on the couch, her temporary bed.

She ran it all back, frame by frame. Another near miss. She'd almost made it. But the smart bastard had outfoxed her. Standing at the fence checking out the trees, she'd expected him to run up on the trail behind her. Then, as he approached, she'd have shinned up a tree. She'd already picked one out, a tree with a stout brunch poking out over the fence. If she'd crawled along it with him below, he'd have had no choice. Her head rolling off her body and dropping at his feet—he'd never allow that. No way. When all he had to do was click a few keys. For sure, he'd have shut down the sensors and tried to recapture her from the other side of the fence. She'd have had a chance. As for his finale, telling her to kill herself and bidding her farewell, that was phony. She'd forced it out of him. She'd dumped pity on him. His impotence. That was like marking it up with a highlighter instead of compassionately reaching out. *That happens to lots of men. It's nothing. You're so stressed is all.* Why was the smart thing to say always so damn obvious on the replay? She'd have to be more careful. Mistakes with this guy could flip him off the edge and who knew where he'd land?

She finished the coffee and wriggled down into the comfort of the sofa, tracking back and forth in her thoughts and always winding up at the same dead end.

What next?

She dozed unintentionally, her mind drifting into quiet. When she woke, it took her a moment to find her place in the world. She'd gotten so used to the apartment. She pulled herself up, rested, but groggy, and listened.

No Ted.

She got up, went out into the hallway, and looked up the stairs. Was he still up there, hiding in his bedroom? She went down the ramp to the basement.

The control room.

The door was closed but she could hear him inside.

She listened at the door. He was talking to someone. No, not talking, or maybe talking, but not to someone. She couldn't make out the words. Talking to himself, most likely, mumbling. She went to the kitchen, took a yogurt from the refrigerator and ate it. She was in the hallway heading back to the lounge when Ted appeared from the basement. He was wearing a windbreaker and a scarf.

"Going out?" she said.

"We need to talk." His voice was gravelly, his eyes wide and empty.

"What about?"

"You're right. This was only ever a fantasy. You'll never be mine." Cass resisted the urge to jump in and nail this line of thinking down hard. This was not the moment to push him too fast or too hard. He was heading the right way now. All she had to do was keep him on track. "Let's sit down. I need to tell you something first."

She led the way into the lounge and sat back at her spot on the couch. He sat opposite in an armchair, a coffee table piled with butterfly books between them. He sat on the edge of the chair, his elbows on his knees, his hands clasped together, like a visitor who's dropped in uninvited and doesn't plan on staying long.

"I've found a way for us to get out of this mess. Both of us. With dignity." She eyed him warily, no idea what was coming. She gave a barely perceptible nod and he continued. "Things have become impossible. But before we get there. I need to—"

"Get where?"

Ted frowned like her interruption had broken his chain of thought. That wasn't a good sign. There was a big speech coming, something he'd thought about long and hard and rehearsed to get right. Something important. That was a worry. The only important thing to Cass was survival. A while back, she would have added freedom to that, but that was when she'd been dealing with a run-of-the-mill kidnapper. Or so she'd thought. Now she knew the truth. Now she knew what was lurking inside him, what was camouflaged by this insignificant little man and his endless apologies. A monster. Forget all those creepy images with ghoulish faces and razor-sharp claws. This was the real deal, not Gothic, but twenty-first century, armed with code not claws, and driven not by a thirst for blood, but by love twisted around insanity and woven into a designer noose. "My solution." He finally found his place. "But before then, I want to tell you the truth. And I want you to hear me out, okay? No more interruptions." Cass swallowed, her throat dry and tight. She managed another weak nod. "I lied to you. Just once. About India. I said that was all I remembered... about your brother. Nothing else. That was a lie. I remember everything. I remember two beautiful American girls, two blue-eyed blondes. One was Cassandra Beauvoir and one was Zoe Lynch." Cass sat up rigid and slid forward, her face blank, shock sucking her thoughts and feelings off into ether.

"How did you find out our names?"

"Long ride, wasn't it? 72 hours to be exact. I wasn't the only one to take a nap."

"You checked our backpacks."

"I wanted to know more about you. I collect things, and things I can't have I photograph. You'd already made it clear I couldn't have you. So I got pictures of you both sleeping and photos of your passports too."

You fucker.

She didn't say it. There were more important things afoot, like what was coming out of his mouth next.

"That day at CoinAxis when I recognized you, I mentioned it to one of their IT guys. I know that girl, I said. Zoe. I met her in India. And he says, no, you got it wrong. Her name's Cass. And my head went..." He twirled his finger around, spinning an imaginary top. Her eyes followed the movement, a siren screeching in her head, the one they played when the nukes were on the way and heading for your house.

"You little fucker." There, she'd said it. But what the hell? That was down to him. He'd opened Pandora's Box. He'd said the Z word. He'd let Zoe loose.

"I was pissed off with you. I was only trying to make polite conversation and you—"

"Creep."

"You were a lot less than polite, especially you, Zoe. But we won't get into that." He waited, but she was done with her protestations. "I remember everything about that ride. Your conversation about art—some painting you'd both seen in the National Gallery—and how your face changed when she told you about her acceptance at the Royal College of Art in London. How your blue eyes turned greener and greener the more she went on about it."

Anger writhed inside her with nowhere to go. She was helpless, and that was the truth of it. He was holding her up with forceps like one of his prize butterflies. He was staring at her naked. Not nude, but unmasked, every cloak she'd ever hidden under torn away.

"Ted, I..." She ran out of breath, the room suddenly airless, its walls closing in, her past looming menacingly. "If you knew that, if you had those photos, then why did you kidnap me? You could have blackmailed me. I'd have..." She trailed off again, no need to state the obvious. She'd have fucked anyone to keep that hidden, even Toady.

"I love mysteries, and there it was. How did Zoe Lynch, the not so posh girl from Charleston, West Virginia, become Cassandra Beauvoir, the very posh girl from Greenwich, Connecticut? I wondered about that... the background thing. Different class. It's still a thing here, but people don't talk about it like they used to. All brainwashed into thinking we're equal. It's bullshit of course. In Oxford, they treated me like I was a slug."

"Where are you going with this? What do you want? I can make nice. Is that it? I can be anything you want me to be."

"No, no. It's never going to work, if I wanted to do that, I could have done it from the beginning. I'm not an animal. I wanted it to be real."

"Then what?"

"The truth. Your truth and mine. Then we can finish this. I wanted to know what happened. So I hired guys—ex-cops—to find out. They followed your trail from India to Thailand, greasing a lot of palms on the way. But then the trail took a weird twist in a fishing village on the coast down by Songkhla. Seems there's a special island down there. Ko something. Not one of the famous ones. No resort hotels or spas. Only way to get there is on an unofficial ferry. Not really a ferry at all, more like a fishing boat. They sent me a photo. All wood. Chinese junk style like in an old Bruce Lee movie. So Cassandra Beauvoir and Zoe Lynch both went to that island by boat, but only Zoe ever came back. And if that isn't wild enough, Zoe shows up in London, years later, magically fulfilling Cassandra's dream and living her life."

"She fell."

"Off the boat?"

"I never pushed her." That stopped him dead. Whatever he'd been expecting, a blundering confession by denial wasn't it, and Cass regretted it as soon as it came out of her mouth. Ted waited, eyes like a hungry gecko watching a fat fly edge closer. "The crossing was overnight and most of the next day. No cabins, no bunks, no seats, just a few benches. We were the only foreigners. We slept on the wooden floor with our backpacks as pillows. There was only one toilet—if you can call it that—and it stank of diesel, shit and men. So we peed over the side. There was no railing, just a knee-high parapet, and at the back of the ship, there was a stack of barrels tied down with a net. So we sneaked behind it and sat on the parapet to do it there. It was scary. Stupid. Sticking our asses out with all that rushing, foamy water a foot away. But with what we'd been smoking, we laughed about it."

"So she fell in and you didn't mention it to—"

"Hey, what do you think I am? She was my friend. I loved her."

"So what happened?"

"A freak wave. Something. I don't know. The boat rocked and she was gone. I told the Captain. There were only five crew. But none of them spoke English. So I couldn't get it across."

"And the police when you got to shore?"

"I tried. It was a real poky little village. I found a cop who spoke a bit of English. While I was writing out a statement for him, he locked the door and grabbed me from behind. I had to fight my way out of the place."

"What about her family?"

"Her parents were dead. No brothers or sisters. No extended family. I knew everything about her. We'd been traveling together for months. Talk, talk, talk. That's all we did."

"So she fell and conveniently left her backpack."

"I planned to go to the US Embassy with it when I got to Bangkok. It wasn't like you're thinking. She fell, and even then I didn't plan to take her identity. Of course not. Who would? There was never any sinister plan. But when I checked her phone—we'd shared PINs for safety reasons—it came to me as I was watching the Zoom interview she did for the Royal Academy. We were hardly twins, but we could have passed for sisters. Same height and build, same coloring. No one looks exactly like their ID photo, and the biometrics chip has just the basic information, digital image, etcetera. Nothing fancy like an iris scan or fingerprints. She already had a student visa. She'd gotten the stamp at a British Consulate in India. All I needed was new hair and different makeup. All the rest could be put down to a year on the gringo trail in South Asia."

"Didn't she have any friends in America? There had to be—"

"I messaged them. Cass was big into yoga. They knew that. So I told them I was—Cass was—adopting Mauna. Know what that is?"

He shook his head.

"A vow of silence. I told them it was a requirement of the monastery I was at, part of my practice to conserve spiritual energy and achieve a higher state of consciousness."

"And they bought it?"

"Two of them even sent me a shushing face emoji, getting into the spirit of it."

"And no trouble at UK border control?"

"Welcome to the UK, Cassandra, I hope your studies go well. All delivered with a big smile. That's all there was to it. A great opportunity dropped in my lap. What was I supposed to do? Throw it overboard after Cass and head back to West Virginia and my own shitty life. That was everything I was running from." She waited for the comeback, the challenge, more accusations. But he was smiling.

"My guess was you'd killed her."

"I'd never... Why would you...?"

"Remember the Indian man who took your seat? You wandered off for a smoke and when you got back, there he was, and however nicely you asked, he wouldn't give it back. So you grabbed his bag and hung it out the window. That got him moving his arse out of the seat double quick. Then you chucked it up the aisle and got your seat back while he was fetching it. Was he ever pissed? You showed him up. A white woman humiliating an Indian man in his own country. I don't know what he said, but I know what waving your fist in someone's face means. But you just sat there, peeling an orange with a knife. Would you like me to cut you a piece, you said, holding up the knife in front of your face so he could get a good look at it. It was like popping a balloon. *Whoosh*. All that hot air blew out of him, and he shrunk to nothing. Yeah, that girl could kill someone. But I didn't give a damn. The way you'd reinvented yourself here in England. The way you'd dropped Zoe and become Cass. That was a magical transformation. Asia was your chrysalis. It was mine too. You know what I'm talking about. When a cocoon cracks open, something beautiful emerges. Something unlike anything that went into it. All I needed to do was create a new chrysalis and put us both in it. This place, that basement, these days together, they're our chrysalis. One day it will crack open and Mr. and Mrs.

Sharpe will emerge." He whimpered, his eyes moist, then wet. "Except it won't. I got that part wrong." He stood up, took off his jacket and unwound his scarf.

The choker!

The Melbot choker.

He was wearing it.

She didn't ask why. She didn't need to. This was the total of everything he'd said. Her fears had become reality. He'd gone off the edge. And now they were both two short words from the end.

"Ted," she whispered, her voice cracking up.

"The fantasy ends now and I set us both free."

"What happened earlier, between us in the grass... you need time is all. I can help you. I promise."

"If I can't live with you, at least I can die with you."

"Why kill either of us? You've got something on me. You don't need this." She touched her choker. "Let me go. I won't tell the police. I can't. I'll come back whenever you want. Just pick up the phone and call. I'll be so nice to you, so gentle, so loving, everything you want me to be. I'm that woman."

She rambled on. Saying what? It didn't matter. None of it registered in his eyes, and that stone dead stare was all the answer she needed. They'd long passed the point of no return. His obsession had sustained him for years and she'd stripped it from him. She'd uncovered his secret, the one he'd buried so deep he'd forgotten it existed. She'd hollowed out his life force. So he'd shared his knowledge of her secret. She knew his, and he knew hers. That was the trade. They were both naked now, staring at each other's core.

"Please, Ted... there has to be another way for us."

Her words hung in the air like a lifeline waving in the wind out of reach. Tears oozed out of his eyes and she did all she could do to stop hers, but then she let them go.

14

Ted's mind zoomed back to his childhood. Odd to think of it at a moment like this, about to die, about to take someone's life. But there it was. Maybe it was part of dying. Maybe it had already begun. The words had not yet passed his lips, but Cass and the rest of the world were getting dim as if sliding behind dark glass. And sounds were getting distant. Her lips were moving, but the words were muffled... *please, please,* something like that, background notes that washed over him and went on their way.

Dark glass... it was stuck in his head.

As a child, he'd always skipped Sunday school. Aunt Nell would dress him and send him on his way, but he'd head straight to an abandoned quarry, a *Huck Finn* landscape of islands and lakes. One day, he'd come across a group of boys smoking and laughing in a wood nearby. They'd invited him to join in the fun. He was thrilled. He'd be one of the lads. But as he coughed his way through his first cigarette, his head in a nicotine spin, they'd turned on him, pointing and accusing.

Girls.

He was at the center of a circle, wilting under a barrage of questions. Who'd he done it with? He fumbled and lied, inadvertently giving them what they wanted, a floor show, someone to bully and beat. Their jeers soon turned into fists, and ragged and bruised, he'd fled. He couldn't go home looking like that, not to his forbidding aunt. So he ended up in Sunday school where there was a toilet to clean up in before going home. Sitting on a bench with anger and hurt frothing under his hooded eyes, he'd read the assigned lesson.

Faith, hope and love. None of it had made sense at the time and he'd never thought of it since. But now it came to him in snippets, *when I became a man, I put away childish things … through a glass darkly*.

From boy to man, this was the end.

Her palms were clasped together, not neatly arranged like they do in churches, but the fingers entwined, squeezed white as if in prayer to the God of last resort. He wiped his face with the back of his hand. It was wet. *I must be crying.* But that wasn't going to stop him. He could do it, find the strength, like the day he'd taken her. He'd stepped up and been a man that day. No, he was reading too much into that. He'd never been a man, not once since the day those boys had outcast him.

He opened his mouth to say the words, the four words that would bring it all to an end. Two for Cass and two for him. He'd have done it already, but timing it right was a challenge. The chokers were two-step devices. They choked first, then killed. His estimate for Cass was five minutes total, with her losing consciousness somewhere between two and three minutes. Something to be grateful for that. When blood came bursting out of her throat, she'd be out cold already. But his choker was a wildcard. He'd sized it for her neck and that hybrid cantaloupe it had taken forever to find. He hadn't recalibrated it. No time. His neck was bigger, not a tree trunk like Superman Washington, but when you're talking about a wire cutting into your throat, a few tenths of an inch is the difference between living and dying. His life would be on a much shorter fuse than hers. He'd have to start her choker before giving the command to his. He'd have to watch her being choked without being distracted if they were to die together. Cass reared up on her knees, still with her hands interlocked, pleading to her deaf-eared God.

Nothing more to be said, but so much to say.

I can do it. But not like that. Heat, sweat, breath.

Then how, she'd say.

Like Thomas Crown… that chess game that went on and on, that endless kiss, heads swirling.

Maybe.

No, that wouldn't work either. Even if he was Steve McQueen and she was Faye Dunaway. It still wouldn't work. It would always end up too real, too frightening.

"Cassbot kill."

Her scream got to him, smashing the dark glass wall. She made a grab for her choker, but he caught her arms. If she got her fingers caught under it, the pain would be brutal, far worse than the terror of choking. They might even get chopped off before she passed out. She fought him, getting her hands free and trying again. But the choker was already too tight. She grasped her throat, shaking her head from side to side.

"Melbot kill."

No going back.

In seconds, neither of them would be able to breathe. In five minutes or less, they would both be lying headless on the floor, decapitated by a guillotine masquerading as designer jewelry. Cass was gasping already, snatching wisps of air and not wasting them on words. She was back behind the dark glass, his vision fading.

Oxygen.

His brain was getting starved of it.

Cass staggered up on her feet.

One last burst.

That had to be the end, the end of her. She crashed the coffee table aside, stumbled and fell on him, pinning him to the armchair. He didn't fight back or struggle. No point. Pain dug deep into his throat and spit dribbled from his mouth. He'd got the timing wrong. Blood was already oozing out of his throat. He'd be gone first. That fat artery in the neck had to be seconds away.

Cass had her arms all over him, her face beacon red, her mouth agape and sucking on empty. She was holding something—it took a moment for it to register—his phone. She'd snatched it from his pocket. She held it up to his face, not so much choking now as whimpering, death coughing up life from deep in her belly. Maybe it was that sound that got to him, that whimper, and something in her eyes, some hope beyond hope. Or maybe it was his own fear of dying switching on some survival circuit buried in the human genome. He watched his robot hand running on reflex, his finger punching numbers. The PIN was easy, pure muscle memory. He could have poked that in from the grave. But the code for the chokers? The emergency release? He'd coded one in for sure.

Cass dropped the phone and fell back on the floor.

Is she dead?

That thought was enough to kick out one last blast of adrenaline.

Life.

Suddenly he wanted it, no why involved, just want.

He jerked the phone up to his face and poked the blurred keys as darkness swept him away.

Hours later, unsure if he was dead or alive, Ted stared at the ceiling. His best guess was dead, and if he was wrong about that, it didn't matter. He surely soon would be. No feelings, no concerns as to living or dying. Wasn't that the same thing? He faded away, and the next time he came to, he stayed conscious long enough to crawl across to Cass. She was lying on the floor a few feet away and the flickering movement of her chest told him what he needed to know. No need to check her pulse, she was alive. He must have deactivated her device somewhere between choke and kill. Her throat was bruised, but not bleeding like his.

He pulled himself up on his knees and explored his wounds with his hands, then looked at his fingers. Blood all right. He deactivated his choker and removed it, then levered himself up unsteadily. Blood trickled from his neck. Another ten seconds and it would have been a gusher. He left Cass to regain consciousness and went upstairs to his ensuite bathroom.

The bloodied Melbot needed washing. But as he turned on the water, he saw himself in the mirror behind the sink.

My neck.

It was way worse than that smear of blood on his fingertips had suggested. These cuts were deep. He hung the choker on the towel rail, took off his clothes and showered, his eyes on the bloodstained water swirling at his feet. Dried off, he daubed his wounds with antiseptic and patched them with Band-Aids. But that proved to be a useless endeavor, and the Band-Aids were soon sopping wet.

I need a doctor.

There was no doubt about that, but there was no way he could go to the local hospital with another gardening accident story. He checked the medicine cabinet and took a few OTC painkillers. He had prescription stuff too, codeine and Valium. But they were risky. He had to avoid anything that would slow him down or mess with his thinking. He was barely keeping up with events as it was.

Setting aside some painkillers for Cass, he dressed and hurried downstairs. He was in the hallway, heading to the kitchen to get some coffee, when he met

Cass emerging from the living room. Neither of them spoke at first. They stood still, staring at each other. There was something different about her, that look on her face. He couldn't put his finger on exactly what it was, but he got the gist of it. She'd changed. She'd been outed as Zoe, a woman with a dark past and a buried secret. He'd dragged her skeleton out of the closet and rattled it before her eyes. Even Rob Washington didn't know her like he did. And likewise, ditto for her. She'd held up a mirror in front of him and...

No, mirrors only see the surface.

She'd run him through a scanner that shot photons into his soul. Yes, something had changed inside each of them, and something had changed between them too. They'd snuck up to death hand-in-hand, poked him in the eye, then done a runner. That would change anyone.

Cass broke the eerie silence. "Thanks for doing the right thing."

He nodded, then said, "Are you okay?" A stupid question, and he could hardly believe he'd said it. "I got you some painkillers." He offered her the plastic strip. "I was about to get some coffee."

She took the painkillers and as she stepped closer, she noticed his neck and her face screwed tight. "That's terrible. It's worse than mine. You should go to the doctor. You need stitches. It could get infected."

He shook his head resolutely.

"There's only one hospital. We're in the country."

"Then go to a pharmacy and get some DIY stitches. They're like strong Band-Aids. Super sticky. Those things won't hold." She pointed at the regular Band-Aids curling and crinkling on his neck. "And iodine."

She was right, of course. But what to do? If he left the house, he'd have to lock her back downstairs. That would be a mistake. There had to be a measure of trust going forward, even if it was underwritten by the constraint of the choker. If he treated her like a prisoner again, they'd lose this special something. He didn't know what that something was, but the feeling was too strong to be denied. Besides, why shouldn't he leave her with the freedom of the house? She couldn't go anywhere and there was no landline in the house. There were plenty of computers and other electronic devices. But they were all locked down. It was technically impossible for her to contact anyone. As for her threat to commit suicide, she'd just chosen life over death. So there was no chance of that. He was wobbling this way and that. But then the clincher pushed him. Cass squeezed his arm, not threatening, but kindly and warm.

"I'll make some food while you're gone."

Ted nodded. There was no way back after that.

"There's a freezer in the utility room. You'll find loads of stuff there."

Saying that felt so good, a real buzz. There they were, Ted and Cass together, like a proper couple, planning a day together. It was his dream piped straight through to reality.

Onward and upward.

He tossed the last of his fears aside and headed for the front door.

15

Cass sat at the kitchen table, fingers drumming silently on its wood, ears pricked as she followed Ted's movements in the hallway and out the door. When it clicked shut, a wave of relief made her shudder, stress oozing out muscle by muscle, her body turning to jelly. Even after he'd gone, she stayed like that. She needed to move, do stuff, think. But however important those things were, this moment had to be taken and enjoyed. Yes, she still had the dog collar on, and she had dodged death by a whisker. But compared to sitting in a five-star jail, sitting in a proper kitchen with no supervision and staring out a window at greenery was glorious. So she savored it, sucking it all in while keeping one eye on the muddled ideas and half-baked schemes streaming through her head. Finally, she reigned in both and forced herself to think hard and straight. She'd been a fool and she'd almost paid the price for it. How could she have been so wrong about him? She'd labeled him as an unstable, obsessive stalker, and he'd proved her right with his stun gun, self-harm spectacular.

But this crazy!

Capable of killing them both.

That was nowhere in her card deck of outcomes.

Coming on to him had been a calculated ploy, floating around in her head for some time, and rolling in the grass, blood hot and breath heaving, there would never be a better moment. The logic driving it made sense. She'd set aside what he said he wanted and gave him what—in her opinion—he really needed. A good fuck. Getting him off would have reworked the landscape between them like a seismic event. She'd have ended up deep inside his head, not banging around half in, half out. She'd have leverage. No problem with that plan. It wouldn't shortlist her as a feminist of the year candidate. But with a pinch of luck and gritted teeth, she could make it work.

Was she to blame for not seeing the roadblock?

Looking back, these things were so damn obvious. Kidnapping a woman, not for sex or money, but to court her. Yes, court, a nice old-fashioned word for a nice old-fashioned boy.

What kind of man does that?

One who has no other option.

Nice old-fashioned boy?

They don't exist.

And after blundering into the roadblock she should have seen coming, she'd doubled down on stupid. Instead of thinking on her feet and comforting him, she'd patronized him, dumping pity on him. Men hated pity. He had a secret he couldn't live with. So he'd buried it in concrete, and she'd used a sledgehammer to set it free, then staged a live theater event to make sure he got the message.

Before this, she'd wondered where the edge of his world was. That mystery was solved. She now had the full measure of him and she'd run out of ruler. Her mind flitted through the slideshow of horrific crimes committed by incels over the years and reported on the nightly news. At the time, she'd skipped past them, paying them little mind. What with the endless wars, climate disasters, and the world's worst human beings ascending to seats of power around the planet, she didn't have enough inside her to care about that too. But now it had gotten up close and personal. Ted was not merely a weirdo—dangerous, but controllable. He was a psycho and she'd be lucky to get out of this place with her life. That reality streamlined her options, leaving her with a simple choice. Play his game and survive or end up on no-way-back boulevard, and she'd already gone down that road as far as she ever wanted to travel.

She glanced around the kitchen, checking for cameras. Nothing visible. They'd be hidden, of course, spycams like in the apartment.

But then again, why?

This was his house, not a jail extension, and in contrast with her apartment's fresh-paint newness, the house was ancient. The basement apartment had been built with surveillance and security in mind from first brick to last. This farmhouse had to be hundreds of years old. There'd be no way to punch holes in the wall and rig hidden cameras without leaving a trace. These walls looked like they'd crumble if you hung a poster on them with a thumbtack. Buoyed by the notion that she was out of the surveillance zone, she explored, checking the utility room. Like the kitchen, all its appliances were new. She looked in the freezer. Lots of gourmet frozen meals to make her offer of fixing dinner an easy task. She went back down the ramp to his control room in the basement, thinking he might have overlooked a phone or some other communications device. She wasn't hopeful. But with blood dripping out of his neck, he might have made a mistake. Nothing. It was just as before. Even on the point of suicide, he'd logged out of all his devices securely. She scanned shelves littered with electronic devices, cameras and accessories. Nothing had changed since she'd peeked through the door earlier.

Unsure how long he'd be, and eager not to waste time, she went back up the ramp, stood in the reception hall next to the ugly horse's head, and double-checked the ground floor. Kitchen, drawing room, dining room, bathroom with WC—she hadn't spent much time in any of them, but enough to know they were poor bets for what she was looking for. There were two other doors, a cozy sitting room with a fireplace and a stack of logs, and under the stairs, a storage closet. She checked the closet—the usual brushes and brooms, a vacuum cleaner, and a set of ancient-looking golf clubs. She pulled one out, a driver. That would make a serious weapon. She dropped it back. They had to be leftovers like the horse's head. She couldn't imagine Ted playing golf. There was something else too. A bat. She pulled it out. A cricket bat, old like the clubs. She left it all as it was, closed the door and headed upstairs.

A quick scouting revealed four bedrooms and three bathrooms, all with their doors unlocked. There was one other room, but its door was locked. Some sort of security door, heavy-duty, probably made of wood but finished with steel plate. Next to it was a glass entry panel like the one at the entrance to the basement. She stood in front of it, wondering what might be on the other side.

Interesting, but inaccessible.

She moved on, picking the largest of the bedrooms first. It was the only one with a lived-in vibe and obviously his bedroom. She didn't know what she was looking for, but this looked like the right place to find it. She took her time moseying around. But there was little of interest in the bedroom itself, so she moved on to the ensuite bathroom. It was well appointed, but oddly ordinary compared to her apartment's lavish setup. Her eyes skimmed over the tub and shower, stopping dead at the towel rail. He'd left the still-bloody Melbot hanging off it. She stared at it for the longest time, fighting the nightmare it triggered, then shook her head to snap out of it. She steadied herself, gripping the edge of the sink grimly with both hands, happy to ignore the ragged face staring back at her from the mirror behind it.

Medicines.

The mirror was the door of a bathroom cabinet.

She opened it.

Having avoided touching anything so as not to leave a trail, here was something she could legitimately touch. He'd given her a strip of ibuprofen downstairs. But she'd been strangled halfway to nowhere, and if that wasn't a bona fide excuse for looking for more painkillers, then what was? She scanned the shelves, blowing a soft whistle. This was the mother lode all right, packed with pillboxes, vials and tinctures. She checked their labels, moving fast. He'd told her they were in the middle of nowhere. So his trip to the pharmacy was sure to take some time, but she wanted to be back in the kitchen when he returned. She was looking for something useful, but useful how? Some of these drugs she'd never heard of.

Mirtazapine, amitriptyline?

If only she knew, she could serve him up an overdose with his dinner. But what sense did that make? The Cassbot gave her a two-week lifespan. She had to keep him alive to change the battery. Killing him would only work if she could disable the sensors.

Electricity.

That was the key.

Get to a junction box, throw switches, pull out fuses, or short-circuit the system. With no electricity, the sensors would be dead. She could climb the fence. Outside the Wi-Fi range, he'd have no remote access to the choker. A specialist could then remove it. She mulled it over. Not ideal. Ted would never leave a single point of failure without a backup. There'd be a hidden generator somewhere. Or else he'd have hacked into a neighbor's system to suck juice from there. Pot farmers were notorious for running indoor grow systems on parasite feeds. Fixing up a failover setup like that would be child's play for Ted. It might work. But who knew? She filed it under potential solutions, a last resort maybe, more of a dice roll than a plan.

Think!

She continued to check labels and contents while shuffling escape angles in the back of her head.

Diazepam.

Now you're talking.

She knew what this one was.

Valium.

There was even a half-empty liquid vial of it. No syringes though. He'd used that to knock her out. So there'd be sweet karmic justice in giving him a taste of his own medicine. She poured a bunch of pills into her hand. Quite a few, but far from a lethal dose. Even if she'd wanted to kill him, these were a poor choice. She'd need way too many. She pocketed a handful—enough for a Mickey, but still with no clear plan in her head—and headed downstairs. Time was running out. She hurried to the kitchen and set to work preparing the dinner. Forget those frozen gourmet meals. She had something special in mind. Still no plan. But she had an idea. It was a fragile one at first, short on detail and riddled with blanks. But as she checked out the stove and prepared what she fully expected to be their last supper together, it grew and grew until it hardened and set.

The great escape, she called it.

Will it work?

Maybe not. But that didn't trouble her. A far more significant obstacle loomed mightily... *do I have the guts?*

16

As Ted secured the outer gate, the phone in his pocket gave a double jolt.

Cyclops... something's up.

That second signal meant trouble. Maybe. His surveillance server sent him an alert if he hadn't logged in for six hours, and if that reminder was ignored, it sent two reminders to signal a twelve-hour period. But critical incidents also got two jolts.

He checked it as he made his way back to the Land Rover and slipped behind the wheel. Everything was okay. He sat back, relieved. It was just the twelve-hour alert. It wasn't Cyclops saying, *Sorry, she was leaving the property. I had to kill her.*

Even though it wasn't the worst news, it wasn't good. Failing to check in with Cyclops was careless, a foolish omission, but in the circumstances, excusable. He checked the logs. He'd been monitoring Washington and his cronies so long, it was easy to identify recordings that might be of interest and those that wouldn't be. Monty's landline to Pix's mobile was one of extreme interest. No one used landlines much anymore, and Monty never called Pix. According to the previous update, Washington was staying at Monty's place. So most likely, it was him. But why had he called on the landline instead of his mobile? Maybe he'd finally caught up with the gravity of his situation. A warrant for his arrest was on the cards. So pretty soon, Ted wouldn't be the only party eavesdropping on his calls.

"Did you book the jet?" Pix's voice was insistent, almost shrill, and she'd used the magic word.

Jet!

They were doing a bunk.

Ted's heart soared. He could play this to Cass. It would tip the balance. She'd see—no question—her relationship with Washington was finished. He was dumping her for Pix and leaving her with a pile of incriminating paperwork implicating her in fraud.

But Ted's face fell when Washington's answer finally came, his voice faltering, circumspect. "I couldn't get through." That stank of lying. "Monty had people here. I didn't have any privacy." Another whopper. "Listen, the cops, did they—"

"Of course they took the bloody laptop. That's what they came here for. That and you."

"Me? They had a warrant for me?"

So this was Washington's follow-up call the morning after his fortuitous trip to fetch a bottle of wine. He'd let her sweat it out alone overnight. Now he was getting the update, Ted was getting the picture, and Pix was getting furious.

"If they had, it would be too late to fly anywhere, all the exits would be blocked. It's now or never. No more wobbling. Book that fucking jet. I went through hell for you. Hours of it. Never again. Next time I'll shoot my mouth off. So you'd better put me on a plane and get me somewhere safe. If you won't book it, I will. It's tonight or never."

Ted liked the sound of that. But Washington's dodging was a concern. He was still making half-arsed efforts to find Cass.

"I feel like shit abandoning her after what happened. If only I could get something to tip off the police, then we could—"

"Like the Rolex man?" Was she teasing? That didn't make sense. They'd already gone down that road and gotten nowhere. They'd even checked employee files to jog their memories. So why was she bringing it up now? "What if I tell you who he is?"

Ted cried out, her snide question like a whippy cane slicing into his butt.

She knows.

"You remembered?"

"Yes and no. Maybe."

Maybe?

Ted buckled over and grabbed the wheel. She'd remembered alright. He could hear the triumph in her voice. Yes, she knew. But she hadn't just remembered. She'd always known. She'd lied to Washington. Of course she had. Why would she help him find Cass? Ted was her secret ally. By sucking Cass into a spaceship and spiriting her off the face of the earth, Ted had done her a favor. They were inadvertent co-conspirators. He had disappeared Cass for her, and now she could disappear Washington for him. At least, that was how it would work out in a perfect world. But where was it going in the imperfect one, the real one?

"Who was it? Come on. Stop playing games." Washington was getting edgy. He didn't like being jerked on a chain. He liked to do the jerking.

"I'm not going to tell you until we're on that jet."

Excellent, Ted thought. That would give him time to vanish with Cass. He knew a guy who could help him with that.

"Seriously? What kind of relationship is this if there's no—"

"I'll call you back."

The line went dead.

Ted gasped, his eyes back on the phone, on the logs. That call was hours ago. There had to be a follow-up. He scrolled through the other entries until he found it. Pix had called him back forty-five minutes later.

"I booked the jet," she said. "Got a pen?"

"I'll remember."

"*Get a pen.*"

That didn't sound like a suggestion, more like an order, and that was how Washington read it. Ted could hardly breathe, his chest frozen with tension as he listened to drawers and cupboards being opened and closed followed by the crinkling of paper.

"Got one."

"And you will be there?"

"C'mon Pix, enough of—"

"I'm sorry, it's just you're such a bastard, and you're not thinking straight."

"And you are?"

"What if she's never found?" A pause, echoing emptiness and dragging on and on. "Don't underestimate me. Those packages you sent to lawyers in Panama and the Bahamas, and just about every other tax-dodge republic on the planet. *Hey Pix, FedEx this, FedEx that.*" Another pause. This one sat there forever too, cranking up the drama and doubling Ted's blood pressure. "I read every damn document."

"So..." Washington spat it out, tough and aggressive, wannabe dismissive, but it sounded tinny and hollow. Pix had his balls in a vise and Washington knew it.

Here comes the squeeze...

"You set up Cass. That's the *so* I'm talking about. So what if she's never found? Or let me switch that around. What if the cops find her and take her on a world tour of her financial assets—the ones she doesn't know about? That's a rhetorical question. She'll go fucking nuts. Now fast-forward to the jury trying to figure out this he-says, she-says mess. So who's lying? Could it be this attractive American woman, an artist with no particular financial chops, or this money shuffling, MBA-crypto whiz kid wanker? *Mmmm...* Get the picture?" Washington had no response. Ted shook his head, hard not to smile. Washington was one of those men who believed his dick always pointed to his North Star and followed it with absolute faith. But Pix was a magnet. She'd skewed its focus, and here he was lost between the poles. "Can we get back on track now?" Pix finished her pitch with a close the deal question that left him no wiggle room.

"You're right. I'm not thinking. Let's make a new start when we get on that jet. What do you say? You and me."

"Okay." She didn't sound too convinced. Understandably, Washington was an accomplished liar, much harder to read than his hapless lover whose connivance was transparent every time she opened her mouth. "Do you remember that ransomware attack? We hired a specialist, an encryption expert. I remember it because you complained about the bill. You said no wonder the bastard can afford a bloody Rolex. Edward Sharpe." Ted groaned, a vocalized blast of air shooting up from his guts. He'd planned for failure, yes, but not like this. This was a disaster off even his worst-case scenario chart. "A squidgy little bastard with dandruff who picked his nose while he worked on the code. His company was called Janus Digital, named after the Roman god of locks, according to their website. But that's gone now. The whole company was swallowed up by some American outfit."

Squidgy?

Ted wasn't sure of its exact meaning but it sounded awful.

"Rob...?"

Washington had gone silent.

"I'm here."

"The airport. You've got the time. You've got the place. This ends today. If you insist, you can tip off the police about Cass when you're out of the firing line, sitting on a beach sipping cocktails. But my advice is don't. As for the offshore documents I read word for word... *I never read them, Officer, I don't know what you're talking about.*"

"I understand. I'll be there."

He sounded more convincing this time. He'd have made a fine actor.

"I'm going to work as usual. But I'll get a headache after an hour or so. Then I'll come back here and grab my luggage. I've already packed. You can pick me up here."

"That's risky. Let's meet at the airport."

"Rob..."

"Don't say it. I'll be there. You can count on it."

Ted stood at the door to the farmhouse, looking at the hand holding the key as he slid it in the lock. It was trembling. He shut both eyes and drew a long breath.

Is she still here? Is everything okay?

When he turned the key, he'd have his answer.

The front door creaked as he eased it open and the smell of cooking—onions sizzling in a pan—gave him his answer. Relief washed over his face as he stepped into the reception hall and leaned back against the door to close it. Not only was she still here, but she was cooking dinner as she'd promised. Yes, the choker was always going to make the staying-or-leaving choice one sided, but that didn't matter. Hearing her there in his house was everything. Whatever it took to make it happen. He tried to put the news bulletin he'd picked up at the gate out of his mind.

A fugitive... I'll be an outlaw.

Washington knew. So what next? Flashing blue lights and sirens? No, if Washington had told the cops, they'd be here already. Washington was a risk merchant. That was his business. Crypto was just a way to collect the money. Risk stocked his cash machine, and he knew how to work it. He'd wait until he was personally outside the jurisdiction of UK law enforcement before contacting them. So why did he press Pix so hard to give him the name now? Did he want to take care of it himself before they got on that plane? That wasn't so easy. Ted had cut his ties to his old business and moved twice. He'd even quit his social media accounts, the lepidoptery forums where he was a God.

"Hey," he called out as he stepped into the kitchen, feigning all the casualness he could muster.

"Hi," Cass greeted him, her voice strained but upbeat.

She was at the stove stirring and she didn't look up. He stopped and stared. If only he'd had his camera. Here was a photo that would end up framed on the wall next to the High Brown Fritillary shot that had made the cover of the American Butterflies magazine. Cass was every bit as breathtaking as that prize-winning butterfly, dressed in a soft, flowing dress that hugged her figure. The sight of her there at the stove swept aside the last of his doubts. She was trying. She was reinventing herself. Of course, she was. She had already assumed another identity by choice. So why wouldn't she do it again? The person he'd snatched—the one they called Cass—had been an avatar, a creation of Zoe Lynch, the shape-shifting maestro hidden within her. Now she was transforming herself anew, emerging from the chrysalis he'd spun in his imagination.

Mrs. Edward Sharpe, your husband is home.

"Smells delicious," Ted said. "I didn't know you could cook." Cass flipped the onions and glanced up at him, one eyebrow raised theatrically.

"I'm full of surprises, aren't I?"

Ted smiled, taking the double entendre with good humor. *Keep the mood going.* That was the order of the day. But it did give him a moment's pause. All of her surprises so far had involved the loss of blood, his blood.

"Here, have a taste." Cass scooped sauce from a simmering pan, blowing on it and offering it to him. "You're about to get a treat, my spaghetti Bolognese. I found the minced beef in the fridge and thought it would be better than another one of those frozen dinners."

"Wonderful." Ted leaned in and sucked in a taste with a whoosh of air to cool it off. "Spag bol. Yummy."

"Did you get the stitches?" Ted held up a paper bag. "Sit down. I'll help you with that. This'll take a while." She wiped her hands on a dishcloth, and as he sat and removed the contents of the bag, she took skintight vinyl gloves from a box and slipped them on. There was a surgical pair of scissors lying handily on the table next to the sutures. Ted's eyes lingered there, then moved on. Cass could snatch them up in a heartbeat and drive them into his throat. The thought flitted through his mind. Officially, he'd put his fears aside, but he'd gotten so used to doubting her it was a reflex now. He cleared his head, running a positive thinking tape to rewire his brain. She'd changed. He had to believe that, or there was no future, no progress to be had. She'd made a choice too. That knockdown drag-out fight with death had changed them both. They'd been reborn. She knew the truth about that scumbag Washington and the extreme lengths and suffering that he, Ted Sharpe, would go through to make her his. He'd proved he was ready to die for her.

Cass worked deftly, nimble fingers squeezing together the cuts in his neck and applying the DIY sutures. Her touch was light, soothing even. When she'd finished, Ted went upstairs to clean up and change his clothes.

Back downstairs, Cass called him into the dining room. She'd laid it out beautifully using all his best tableware. They sat down to eat and she served up the salad. It was always going to be a nervous affair, but as they pecked at the food and drank the wine, small talk and trivia shielded them from the dark chasm between them. And by the time they'd made it to the pasta, enough wine had been downed to loosen up the conversation. It was still a long way from the happy couple scene of his dream, but it was pointed in the right direction. After dinner and a joint effort to clear the table, Ted commandeered the kitchen cleanup while Cass made them tea. She chose chamomile, but Ted stuck to his usual Earl Grey with milk and heaps of sugar. Chores done. Ted proposed a tour of his collection.

They wandered around the house, sipping their teas. Ted's collection had two elements—photographs and specimens. His photographs decorated walls in every room, even adorning the staircase. So, as they ascended, they stopped every few steps to admire one. Upstairs, Ted led her to the steel door she'd found on her foray earlier that day. He stuck his palm on the glass panel and the door popped open.

"My specimen room," he said. "My pride and joy." He led her into the room and stood at its center, sweeping his arm in a circle like a conductor honoring his orchestra. "It's really something, isn't it?"

Cass nodded, her eyes scanning the room, her face registering nothing. Ted wondered what she might have been expecting behind that reinforced door. One thing was certain. This wasn't it.

He went to the first display case. It was mounted on the wall and housed an impressive array of colorful butterflies.

"Mahogany." He ran his fingers over its dark wood frame. "Hard to get these days." He pointed to the specimens behind the glass. "There's a lot more to this than you'd think. They're not just organized in scientific order. There's an aesthetic thing going on here. As an artist, you can appreciate that. Like here..." His finger flipped back and forth between two butterflies. "I put the Blue Morpho, all those vibrant colors, next to the Monarch. See the contrast?"

Cass nodded again but said nothing. She was standing between two directional LEDs, low-intensity natural lights designed to avoid damaging the specimens and show off their colors. But they weren't doing her any favors. After the food and wine, she'd looked healthy and flushed. Now she was zombie pale like all the blood had drained from her face.

Ted pressed on, pumping up his enthusiasm to get her attention. He guided her to a workbench in the center of the room. "My spreading board. This is where I prepare specimens for display. I use forceps. There's different positions, so you need to be careful how you spread them. The wings are delicate. It's not just sticking a pin through them like in the old days. I use archival adhesive tape. I start them off in a relaxing jar, so their muscles ease out nice, then use entomology pins."

He broke off. Cass looked super pale. It could be the lighting, or it could be the ethyl acetate he used to euthanize the specimens. He liked the smell—sweet and fruity, like ripe pears or apples. So he didn't bother too much about ventilation. Breathing in the fumes could irritate the eyes and nose. He'd read that somewhere, and something about neurological damage. But they said that about lots of stuff, including most household cleaners. It had never bothered him, and the door was wide open. So it was probably just the lights.

"These are my specimen drawers, my treasure trove." He left her by the workbench and stood by a chest of shallow drawers. "Climate-controlled, of course, made of cedarwood. Funny that. It's because cedarwood repels pests. Keeps insects out. Funny, eh?"

Cass wasn't laughing.

"I need to sit down."

"Here you go." He pulled a chair out from under the bench.

"Somewhere else."

He took her hand and led her out of the room. He went to go downstairs but she stopped him. He kept hold of her hand as she took deep breaths. If they'd stayed like that all night, it would have suited him fine. Gradually, the color came back in her cheeks and she took back her hand.

"I'm okay now. Maybe it was the chemicals you use to—"

"Why don't we watch TV instead?"

She nodded and he turned to go downstairs, but she stopped him, reaching out and touching his arm. "Don't you have a TV in your bedroom?"

"In my..." he spun back. He'd heard it correctly. He was sure of that. But what did it mean?

"I need to lie down. Today has been..." She signed off on the rest of that with a shake of her head.

"I've got a great TV there, a huge one."

"Would it be all right if we did that? Watch some TV. Could we be friends for once and share the night there? As friends, I mean. I don't want to sleep downstairs after what happened today."

Ted agreed readily. That couldn't be better. What a blessing that choker was. Without it, there was no way he could have shared a room with her overnight, and she was right. So much had happened today. It was like 10 years of events minified and stuffed into a single day. He was exhausted too and the wine was spinning his head. For a scary moment, he'd thought she'd meant a roll between the sheets. This was not the player-ready moment for that. But lying together on the bed watching TV, that was perfect.

Cass headed downstairs to change out of her dress and he went to his bedroom. The wine had gone to his head, or maybe it was the wine in combination with all the excitement. Understandable after a day like this. He slipped off his jacket, kicked off his shoes, and sat on the bed with the remote. Netflix had a recommendation for Ted, a documentary on how to live to be 90 plus. He clicked the play button. Maybe that would work for them both, something neutral. Cass hated romcoms. He knew that much from his stalking days. She didn't go for sappy stuff. She liked a good thriller. But not tonight. Not after a day like this. They'd both overdosed on thrills. Live to be 90 plus. Why not? The choice didn't matter because he was planning to take a shower and change into silk pajamas, the same brand as that footballer wears in his TikTok videos. He sorted the pillows at his back. Yes, this was how it was going to be. He'd been man enough to see it through. Taking her had been a crazy act, but he'd done it. And the crazy ride since had almost cost him his life more than once. But they'd both survived and here they were, sharing the same bed.

Washington can jump on his jet with....

Ted's eyes eased closed with a brief stutter like a theater curtain falling at the end of the last act.

17

Cass poked her head through the bedroom doorway.

Ted was out cold, propped up by pillows, shuttered eyes aimed at a TV documentary about how to live forever or something like that.

Perfect.

The Mickey was working. Delivering the Valium in sufficient quantities had involved guesswork and depended on his habits. During her years in the UK, Cass had learned a lot about Brits. They loved an after-dinner cuppa and she'd counted on him being no exception. Sure enough, he'd accepted her invitation without a second thought. Even better, his choice of brew was the flavored and aromatic Earl Grey tea. With two sugars spooned in on top of that, he was never going to taste the crushed pills she'd dumped in it.

Earlier in the day, she'd filled her shopping cart, the one in her head, stuffing it with useful items as she checked cupboards, opened drawers and prepared the dinner. So with Ted comatose, now was the time to head for the checkout.

She hurried downstairs, fetching the duct tape and rope from the utility room first, then stopping at the cupboard under the stairs. This was a tossup—the offensive option—cricket bat or golf club? After some thought, she grabbed the cricket bat and took the stairs back to the bedroom two at a time.

Ted hadn't budged a flicker. But how far out of it was he? What if he'd just dozed off? For her plan to work, she had to manhandle him. Not too much, but the prospect of him coming back to life with a jolt halfway through the procedure and screeching commands at the Cassbot was a worry. She'd need to run a few tests first. She laid out the spoils on the bed next to him, but kept hold of the bat, just in case. Then she squeezed his thigh.

No reaction, nothing, no twitching forehead or tense muscles.

She did it again, harder this time.

Still nothing.

Now for the big decision.

What first?

Tie his hands or tape his mouth?

She leaned the cricket bat against the wall within easy reach. She knew nothing about England's national sport. But she knew how to whack a guy with a baseball bat. The cricket bat was way different, but it would do nicely. It had a long round handle covered in nonslip rubber, easy to hold and shock absorbent. Plus, the bat end was heavy and flat. So she had a choice of striking surfaces, the flat part or the edge. Brought down with her full body weight, that edge would break a bone like a dry twig. So its proximity during this delicate first phase was a reassuring presence.

She set to work. The duct tape was industrial quality and after a couple of loops around his head, she was satisfied that even with his hands free, he wouldn't be talking to the Cassbot anytime soon. Binding the hands was trickier. She needed them strapped tight against his body and that meant rolling him side to side to pass the rope around him. But the more he was trussed, the more she relaxed. Bit by bit, control was passing to her. His power index was waning and hers was waxing. That made it easy to ignore his groans and splutters.

Mouth taped and arms trussed, she took a moment to double-check her handiwork, standing at the foot of the bed with her hands on her hips.

So far, so good.

She was all set. When he came to, she'd move on to the second phase—threatening him with the bat. Just the finishing touches remained. His legs. She couldn't have him getting up off the bed. So she roped his ankles together and tied them to the bedframe. Satisfied with her work, she pulled up a chair and sat on it, staring at him like an anxious relative at a hospital bedside.

Now, it was only a matter of time. All she had to do was play this right. It should be easy. But she knew it wouldn't be. It never was. Hers was the hard road, her karma, as they called it in India. Real Cass had droned on and on about karma, and some of it made sense to Zoe. Today's choices shaped your tomorrow. No question. But the morality stuff was a crock. Perpetrators of evil often benefited almightily, while good Samaritans routinely got shafted. Only a cockeyed optimist would think it was anything other than the algorithm of a fucked-up world.

What did I do to get that mother and father?

If it hadn't been for her brother standing between them, Lord knows what her old man would have done to her. But everything had changed on that fishing boat in Thailand. The red carpet had rolled out every step of the way since. She hadn't only switched identities— she'd swapped karmas. At least, until this detour into Ted's farmhouse basement. But now she had a chance to flip it one-eighty, to get back on the red carpet. All it needed was a few good calls.

Her eyes fluttered closed, then opened. Ted looked to be out for a long count. So she lay on the bed next to him and soon fell asleep.

The midsummer dawn came early in England, but Cass beat it by a good hour. Ted was still in a deep slumber. She went downstairs to the kitchen, brewed coffee and returned with a cup, sipping it slowly, staring at him, dampening down the bubbling heat inside her. As his captive, rage had been a waste of energy. But with the tables turned and Ted at her mercy, a visceral tide of anger was seeping up in her belly. Not good. She had to stay focused. All she wanted was the PIN to his phone and any others she needed to deactivate and remove the Cassbot.

His head shifted from side to side as though he was looking at something passing by. His eyes were still closed, but they were swimming around under the lids. Checking out something in a dream, maybe. REM stage. That meant he was waking up.

Enjoy those dreams, pal. The alarm clock from hell is sitting here with a bat.

She plucked it off the wall, laid it across her thighs and looked up as his eyes fluttered open.

A squeal.

She could only imagine. That was a big gulp of data even for Ted's brain to process in one go—waking up gagged and trussed with his collared and compliant Stacy sitting there with a cricket bat.

He writhed and wriggled.

Cass waited, impossible not to get a buzz out of this.

"Get it out of your system," she said, echoing his words from that first day when she'd woken up in the basement.

She let it go on for a while before giving him a poke in the ribs with the bat, a sharp one to tune him in to the new power dynamics here.

"I'm feeling good, so I'm going to offer you a deal. You don't deserve it, but there it is. I'm all heart." He settled down, laser beam eyes hacking into her. "I'm not going to report you to the police. I don't want you"—she mimed a mouth talking with her fingers and thumb—"blabbing about Thailand." She shrugged theatrically. "I've got something on you and you've got something on me. So we're square. All I need from you"—she plucked his phone off the nightstand—"is the PIN. I'm going to deactivate and remove the choker, then get on my way. If you refuse to give me the PIN..." She put his phone back on the nightstand, stood up and raised the bat up over her head like she was about to split a log.

"Whack, whack, whack!" She sang it out loud and clear, then leaned the bat against the wall and sat down. "Of course, that's not going to happen. You're way too smart." She picked up the phone. "So here we go. No, I'm not dumb enough to remove the tape from your mouth. I'm going to call out numbers from zero to nine. You shake your head for the wrong number and nod when I hit the right one. Then we'll move onto the next number. Got it?"

He nodded, unexpectedly agreeable, and that's how it went. She called the numbers and he nodded on cue. The PIN was 2568. She'd misjudged him. She hadn't planned on it being this easy.

She poked in the number.

Incorrect PIN.

You have two more attempts.

His eyes narrowed, radiating wrinkles.

Was that a smile?

The gleam of defiance in them was unmissable.

She picked up the bat.

"This is my take on Lady Justice. No sword or scales available, so the bat will have to do." She touched him on the shin with it. "This is where justice gets served, right here where there's a juicy nerve." She raised the bat over her head like it was an ax and she was about to split a log. "Last chance."

He grunted, eyes daring her.

She could see it all, her body snapping over, the bat cleaving the air like a samurai sword, the sickening crack as it bit into bone, and Ted... what a performance he'd put on, jerking and writhing, his mangled cry trapped inside by duct tape squeaking out of his throat.

So how come she couldn't do it?

He deserved it. He'd kidnapped her. He'd doped her and knocked her around. He'd humiliated and degraded her. And so what if he hadn't raped her? No Brownie points for that. If he could have, he would have. A slide deck of motivational images flipped through her head. There were reasons aplenty for bringing the bat down with every muscle in her body driving it, getting the satisfaction, hearing his bones crunch, purging her pain by witnessing his. But there it was. She'd turned to Jell-O, some magical shield inside her blocking the blow.

A compassionate heart... was that it?

Where did that come from?

She'd sliced into his thigh till it spurted blood. So what was the problem with whacking him with a cricket bat? She turned away and leaned with one hand on the wall, a string of expletives scorching through her head.

He's a trussed turkey now.

It had to be that. Back then, he'd been armed and a direct threat.

She sighed and let it go, skipping the psych exam. The whys and wherefores didn't matter. It was what it was, a stone wall blocking the emergency exit.

She went to the bathroom, ran cold water and doused her face with it over and over. Bent over the sink watching the water gurgle away down the drain, a new plan came to her, one she was sure she could follow through on.

What if I run a bath, drag him in here and keep dunking him till he cracks?

Waterboarding... guaranteed effective, certified by the CIA.

She shook the last of the water from her hands, excited by the new idea, but not for long. When she reached for a towel, a better one popped into her head.

The Melbot.

It was hanging right there on the towel rail.

She'd seen it earlier on her walkabout when Ted was at the pharmacy. It had been covered with blood then, but he'd cleaned it up since. He must have left it there to dry.

It was potentially a great solution. But would it work?

The answer hinged on the camera. She'd seen an expensive-looking model in the control room. Had he used it to record the Melbot demo? If the recording was still on the camera, maybe she could play it. Cameras weren't set up like computers or smartphones with obligatory passwords and pins. If she could run that video...

She snatched up the Melbot and took it into the bedroom. Ted had calmed down and was leaning back on the pillows propped against the wall. With all that damage to his throat, he must have swallowed a handful of painkillers. That and her Mickey had to be slowing him up. His hooded eyes followed her movements as she fitted the Melbot around his neck. He hadn't figured it out yet, but he soon would.

If only...

She ran downstairs, her feet dancing over the steps, and trotted down the ramp to the basement. Minutes later, she was back in the bedroom, sitting next to the bed. She thumbed the camera controls and looked up at him when she found the video, a broad smile on her face.

Ted's eyes widened.

"So... no more cricket. I have a far more elegant solution, and one I won't need to explain to a smart boy like you." She wiggled the camera.

He grunted, eyes rolling in their sockets.

Dear Ted... what goes around comes around.

She leaned closer until their eyes were inches apart. "You're a smart man, and my terms are simple, generous even. By rights, you should go to jail. You're undeniably dangerous. But you're pathetic too. Plus, I owe you for the heads up on Rob, for letting me know what a shit I was getting hitched to. And something else... for helping me find out who I really am. Yes, Zoe's back. And boy, is she ever glad she kept her passport. I never really enjoyed being Cass. Sure, the money I liked. But as for the rest of it, I went from being stuck in Rob's trophy cabinet to getting pinned under glass on your wall. Maybe the real Cass could have lived with that, but not me. So here's the deal. You abducted Cass, and she's going to disappear for good, leaving Zoe to head off into the sunset with several million dollars of your money, clean money with no links to Rob, Cass, CoinAxis, or any of that crap. This will work for both of us. I end up rich and free. You, meanwhile, can prowl the streets, looking for another victim. Saying that won't get me on the front cover of Ms. Magazine, I realize that, but like I give a fuck. You might try Woolworths. Wasn't that where your movie hero got lucky?"

She picked up his phone, letting it all sink in.

"Last chance saloon."

Ted was smart. He had to see the sense of this. But no. The answer was right there in the willful bastard's eyes.

She put the camera on the nightstand and leaned in close, their faces inches apart.

"You don't think I've got the balls, do you?" She grabbed his hair and yanked him closer. "What if I lied?" She shoved him back roughly and his head smacked against the wall. "I'm talking about Cass. What if I killed her? That's what you thought... the way I brushed off that Indian man on the train. What if you were right? There she was sitting on the parapet, pissing into the shark-infested Andaman Sea and rattling on about her glorious life—*I'll be in the Royal College... blah blah*. Maybe it was too much for me, all the things she'd had given to her for free and all the things I'd had taken from me at a cost, like two accounting columns that didn't balance, hers overfunded, mine in the red."

She leaned back in the chair.

"I said she fell in. But things are not so much what they are as how you look at them—that's what I always say—or how you remember them. And in this case, my memory is wobbly. She did slip. It's true. But when I tried to save her..." She shrugged. "My hands were wet, and on a rocking boat, a clumsy grab can easily turn into a shove. So was that a Tom Ripley moment? You're an old movie buff. You remember Tom." She waited, eyes on his implacable stare. "Talking of old movies, the 60s are done and dusted. I'm not going to end up buried under a tree like Miranda in *The Collector* and I'll do whatever it takes to make sure of that. Just so you know."

Not a flicker of give. She was talking to a wall. She snatched up the notepad and pencil from the nightstand and slid them onto the bed under his right hand.

"The PIN... get writing."

Ted wriggled his back off the headboard and sat forward. She sat next to him and thumbed the camera controls, squeezing up close and angling the screen so they could both see it.

The choker demo video rolled...

He squealed and his body stiffened.

There he was in the field again, next to a table with a melon mounted on a stand, the Melbot looped snuggly around it. "Let's hear what you have to say." She turned on the speakers. "Better get writing."

She'd timed it perfectly.

Melbot activate.

Ted's body convulsed as the red light flashed on his choker.

Now let's say the melon misbehaves. For example, I asked the melon a question politely and it turned its back on me, ignoring me. That's very rude. I don't like rude.

Ted gawked at his on-screen persona as it crossed its arms and stared back at him aggressively.

Melbot choke!

Ted made a grab for the pen. But with his hand tied to the side of his body, her instructions turned out to be overly optimistic. The pen slipped out of his hand and under his leg. He tried to grab it, but that only drove it further underneath him. His guttural squeals punctuated the nails-on-chalkboard whine of the two chokers, the video version on-screen and the for-real Melbot around his neck.

Cass worked double time at the camera controls. She had to stop the audio before it got to the kill command or they'd both be doomed.

On screen, Ted was bragging about his wonderful creation.

Custom-sized... this one for the melon, of course. The Cassbot for you. Yummy, Honey Bun cantaloupe, they call this ... Just about the same size as your neck.

That's when it hit her. She'd blundered... the same size *as your neck,* not his. Their near suicide had demoed that fact in graphic detail. He'd ended up with stitches, but all she'd suffered was bruising. Ted's neck was a long way from rugby Rob's tree trunk. But he'd use that dinky hybrid melon because both chokers were calibrated to fit her. She cut the sound. But surely it was already too late. She grabbed the pen from under his leg and stuck it in his hand. His glow-red face was turning blue, not even a stifled gasp squeezing past the tightening tourniquet at his throat.

He scrawled on the pad.

Was it writing, or the nervous spasm of a dying man?

She snatched his phone off the nightstand and aimed his fingers at the number pad.

It had worked before.

But not this time.

Blood hit her face. She yelped and stumbled off the bed.

Blood and more blood. It squirted through the butterflies and flowers of the choker until the squirt became a dribble and his head lolled onto his chest.

She put her hands to her face, covering her open mouth and shielding her eyes. When she lowered them, it was over. He was still. She looked at her bloody hands and wiped them on her shirt. She stood like that for the longest while. Numb. No thinking, no concern for the consequences of this moment, her thoughts and emotions wiped clean by the spectacle.

The scene still vivid, imprinted in her retinas, she went to the bathroom and washed her hands, reality creeping in on her bit by bit. She stared at herself, her face still bloody.

So was that her future too... blood gushing from her throat?

If she tried to get past that front gate now, it would be.

Unless...

She went back to the bed and searched for the notepad, trying to keep her eyes off Ted. But there was no chance of that. So she bit the bullet, shuddering as her eyes crept up his bloodsoaked belly to his throat and his oddly comical grimace of pain, his eyes glassy with emptiness. He might have been a prop in a horror movie. Surely he'd never been alive. She found the notepad. It was stained with blood, but there were numbers there all right. She sat on the bed and studied them.

5832.

But was that a five or an eight?

She'd already used one of the three PIN attempts. 5832 was her best guess. But it could have been 8832 or 5882. She stared and stared, but there was nothing else for it. This was always going to be a lottery. She punched 5832 into the phone.

Incorrect number.

Her mind raced ahead. What if the last shot was wrong? The phone would nuke itself, erase its contents.

What then?

All she could come up with were pathetic one-liners. *There's plenty of food in the freezer. Someone is bound to come eventually.* She'd already mooted the idea of cutting electricity to neutralize the sensors and rejected it. But she could revive it, look into it at least.

A better option would be to set fire to the house and wait outside in the garden for the fire brigade. Someone had to come then. Of course, that might open the tricky *who is Cass Beauvoir topic*. Stories involving Americans that made the news internationally ended up getting noticed back home, if not on TV, then on social media. Not good. She paced from one side of the bedroom to the other, glancing toward the mess on the bed from time to time, but somehow distancing herself from it the more she walked. In the end, all she could get out of her endless speculation was that doing nothing was always the worst choice, and that was exactly what she was doing.

She sat on the bed.

Hail Mary.

She keyed in 8832, heart hammering. No logical reason for that choice. She just liked the double eights.

She yelped—"I'm in"—turning to Ted as if giving him the update and quickly looking away.

Cass was a long way short of having Ted's tech chops, but with her digital arts training, she had no trouble navigating systems and apps. So after finding the choker app, it wasn't difficult to deactivate the Cassbot and remove it. She was eager to wash the blood off her face, but there was something else she wanted to do a lot more. Searching for the choker app, she'd noticed five banking icons. She clicked the one with Swiss in its title. It prompted her to use facial recognition or enter the PIN. She made a note to set up facial recognition after washing the blood off her face and entered the PIN.

"Shit." She jumped to her feet. "That can't be right." There were several accounts, some cash, others different investment types. Lots of details. But what caught her eye was the total in US dollars based on the current exchange rate of the Swiss franc. She used her fingernail to count the zeros in case she got it wrong. "Holy shit." She logged out, slipped the phone into her pocket and went into the bathroom. She ran the tap, staring at the blood on her face and the grin that burst out beneath it.

18

Rob paced back and forth in Monty's living room, his excitement tempered by anger. The breakthrough—Edward Sharpe—was exciting, but his anger wasn't pointed in that direction, but at Pix. She'd obviously known the identity of the kidnapper all along. She hadn't remembered it *just now*. She'd remembered it way back when he'd told her about the video and the Rolex and asked her to check back through the HR files. She'd been working for IT at that time. She'd had dealings with Sharpe. In fact, she'd been tasked with the job of finding an expert, getting the guy who could dig them out of the hole. Rob had appointed her as his PA later, after a few boozy lunches followed by a stopover at a local hotel. Yes, she'd known from the getgo, but she'd said nothing, banking the info until she could pull it out and trade it for what it was worth.

Don't underestimate me.

She'd made a big point out of that.

So how had he estimated her?

She was a great PA, loyal, smart, and suspicious of everyone. Then there was the rest, the extracurricular shenanigans. She was irresistible. Monty was right. She'd changed him. She was crack cocaine in lingerie. Balling her had started out as a bit of fun and snowballed into chronic addiction. His thoughts hit a wall...

Fuck.

She'd read those documents and that wasn't all. She'd have copied them too. She'd have pulled out her iPhone, fired up the scanner app and click, click, click. She hadn't mentioned that. She'd save that for later like the Edward Sharpe memory glitch. He sat at Monty's computer and logged in with a guest account. He'd be damned before he'd let a woman tell him what to do.

Edward Sharpe?

His plan was simple, no big decisions yet. He had time. Pix was busy. She had to get to the office, fake her headache, get back to the flat, grab her suitcase and make it to Stansted Airport. It wasn't all the time in the world, but enough for him to explore his options, starting with where this bastard Sharpe might hang out.

His first port of call was Companies House, where all UK companies are registered. Janus Digital Ltd had been sold. Before that, Edward Sharpe had been its CEO and principal shareholder with a residential address that tracked to a law firm. The company itself had disappeared, swallowed up by a big player in online security. Sharpe had not been a part of the deal. He'd taken the money and disappeared from the commercial world. Social media wasn't much help either, no Instagram account replete with selfies. But he had left footprints. Everyone does. Outside of cybersecurity, his big thing was butterflies. He'd even won photographic competitions for his shots, although his profile in that area had dwindled over the past few years. But nowhere was there any sign of where he lived.

Rob checked his watch. He still had time, but time for what? And what would happen when the time ran out? Would he be on that jet? He set the decision aside, still too angry with Pix to think straight. He searched the net again with queries focused on a photographic competition Sharpe had won, wading through forums where butterfly geeks talked shop, then moving on to formal societies and associations dedicated to lepidoptery. Who'd have thought it? An entire butterfly world online. Finally, he got lucky—a photograph of Edward Sharpe holding a framed copy of a magazine cover featuring his prize-winning photo of a High Brown Fritillary, Britain's rarest butterfly.

That's it...

The Rolex. It was gleaming right there on his wrist.

Rob checked it against the clip from his neighbor's CCTV video. It was the same, a Cosmograph Daytona Rolex, a more recent edition of the classic made famous by Paul Newman. Better yet, it was the exact model in rose gold.

What are the chances?

These two photos would be more than enough for the cops. He leaned back from the keyboard and stretched his arms. Great, but not so great. If he gave the info to the police, they'd trace Sharpe with a few clicks of a mouse button. They'd have a squad car there in minutes. But how would that go in practice? What would be the ABC of it all? He'd call the cops and say... *My wife was abducted ... last week ... I understand I'm reporting it a bit late, but I've been busy. Anyway, I've solved the case for you. The perp's name is Edward Sharpe. All you have to do is arrest him and rescue my wife. And by the way, keep this to yourselves. Especially, don't share it with your mates at the Serious Fraud Office.* That done, he'd be free to hop on a plane with Pix and live happily ever after.

He stood up and paced the room, then stood at the window, peering down at the street below. Parked cars, plane trees, a woman hurrying along, glimpses of her as she scurried between the trees. He followed her with his eyes, something itching in the back of his head, an idea emerging, not yet clear.

That photo.

Rob checked his watch again. Sooner or later had turned into now. He tried to talk himself out of it.

Just take the jet.

Why not? In hours, he'd be dozing in soft leather with Pix snuggling up against him and an endless blue horizon beckoning through the window. Of course, there'd be baggage, not in the hold, but in his head. He'd be abandoning Cass. He'd be the perfect moral bankrupt, bank account full of cash, heart full of empty.

He went back to the table and called Monty.

"I found out where Cass is," he said as soon as he heard Monty's voice. It was a lie, or generously put a half-truth, but he had to take control of the conversation and steer Monty away from another moralizing lecture about what a louse he was.

"Where?"

"Edward Sharpe has got her." Rob explained how he'd positively identified Sharpe as the abductor, although he skipped any reference to Pix. He didn't want to kick off a debate about that topic again. "But I've got no address. All I've got is a bunch of photos he's taken. Any ideas?"

"I already told you my idea. Tell the police. They'll find him in an instant." Rob said nothing. This conversation was heading towards a replay of the confrontation they'd had the night before. "You still want to play detective, eh?"

"Photos I take on my phone have the GPS location embedded in them. So I was wondering if I could dig out the location data from these photos and find out where they were taken. I thought if anyone could help me with that, it's you." That wasn't idle talk. Before he'd been kicked out of Uni, Monty had been a straight-A student majoring in computer science. "One of these photos is of a rare butterfly he took close to his house. It says so in the caption, and I was thinking—"

"EXIF data. Depending on the camera and how it's set up, there could be all sorts of information. Location coordinates for sure. Where did you get the photo?"

"Facebook, I think. I don't remember."

"No chance. All that data gets stripped on the big social media platforms. If you're serious about playing detective, find a photo on some amateur blog or specialist forum. Location information is important for wildlife photographers. So you might get lucky."

"Thanks, Monty. I'm leaving now, and just so you know, I'm going to do the right thing. That guy you knew, you still know him."

Rob signed off on the call, upbeat now. Monty's info gave him hope, and beyond that, he'd repaired the bridge between them. Monty was the closest thing he'd ever had to a brother and their bumpy exchange the night before had left him unsettled.

Increasingly refined searches led him to a forum frequented by hardcore lepidopterists, men—and they did all seem to be men—who lived and breathed butterflies. Sharpe had been a regular poster on the forum, but in the past year or two, his contributions had dribbled to nothing. Rob finally got lucky with a different photo, an orangey-brown butterfly called a Pearl-bordered Fritillary. According to the coordinates buried in the metadata, it was taken in East Sussex near Abbotts Wood, a rural area between Hailsham and Polegate. Rob checked the satellite photos. Eight properties in the area fitted Sharpe's *almost in my back garden* description. Three of them were bona fide farms. So he set them aside. Farms that size had employees, people who'd notice if a young woman was screaming at the window of a locked tower. Besides, Sharpe was no farmer. He was a hacker who'd gotten lucky with the right skills at the right time and place. That was all it ever took to get rich.

Concentrating on the five remaining properties, he logged in to a title search service with access to the land registry and worked through the first three on the list. No Sharpe. But the fourth got him excited even before he checked the records. It was an isolated property on a deadend track off a lane barely wide enough for a tractor. On the satellite photo, its outside pool looked new, and there were several other buildings not in keeping with the centuries-old farmhouse. This had all the signatures of a serious money upgrade. The Manor, Bluebell Drive. That was the address. A house with no number. No need. It was the only house on the road. He was so confident he was already smiling by the time the name popped up on the screen.

Edward Sharpe.

Rob copied all the information on his phone and headed for the door where he stopped, his hand on the bolt.

Weapons? Tools?

Should he grab something?

He shrugged it off and went through the door. He wasn't going to need anything to take care of Sharpe. He'd taken Cass. Rob had no doubts about that, and no need for weapons either. He'd rip this bastard to pieces with his bare hands and if he'd hurt Cass, he'd find a nice hole to bury him.

He sat in the Bentley and checked the best route. Hop on the M4, pick up the M25, loop south around London, then blast down the M23 and exit onto the A23. According to the app, it would take one hour and forty-five minutes to cover the 88 miles. Rob fired up the Continental GT. He thumped the duo-tone hide steering wheel with the palm of his hand and stabbed the throttle with his foot, relishing the throaty roar of the 6.0 liter engine. "Come on, Duke,"—he said to the car, pausing to grind his teeth—"let's do this. One hour tops." He checked his watch and ran the calculation. It was doable. He could check the farm, and if she wasn't there—if it was a bust—he could still make the jet.

Getting out of the city was—as it always was—a blood-pressure boiling pan of frustration. He'd have been better off on a bike, one of those electric ones. Plenty whizzed past him as he idled in traffic, the sleepy purr of the Duke's monster engine irritating him more with each passing minute. But all that was okay. He'd make up time on the M23, the motorway down to the south coast. It wasn't a bad plan, but it had a lot of ifs. Dependencies, they'd called them in college. He'd aced that module: *Coping with Dependencies, Managing Risks with Coping Solutions*.

Two hours later, he was sitting in traffic on the M25, pounding the Duke's duo-tone hide steering wheel with his fists. Officially known as the London Orbital Motorway, the capital's ring road was better known as Britain's biggest car park. Rob cursed, not complaining to God, this was not an act of the Almighty, but a truck driver whose massive rig was skewed diagonally across three lanes. It had five or six cars crunched into it, and umpteen police and emergency response vehicles completed the chaotic picture he was creeping towards. No, this was not God's fault, and the truck driver was not the only one to shoulder its blame. Mostly, it was down to Rob. Yes, he'd aced Risk Management. But he was a chancer to his core and this was a chance too far. The motorway route promised big savings in time, but trusting the M25 with a life or death mission had always been a roll of the dice. With all the counterclockwise lanes blocked, other than the Duke sprouting rotor blades, bashing the steering wheel was the only coping solution he could come up with.

A trickle of cars was filtering off via the hard shoulder, and Rob worked his way into the line of vehicles finding their way to freedom. But by the time he was cruising, it was over. He'd never make that jet. Pix had texted him throughout the day, updating him as she'd worked through her part of the plan. She'd signed off the first one—*Leaving work now. No probs*—with three emojis, fat red lips, the most recent—*Answer me, you fucker*—with a fat middle finger. Rob muted the phone. He couldn't handle her. Not now. He'd get back to her after checking out the farmhouse. She'd be okay. Stuck in traffic, he'd had plenty of time to figure out an excuse and he'd taken a photo of the accident as evidence. The tricky part was its location on the wrong side of the city. Pix was waiting for him at Stansted Airport, north of London, and here he was way to its south, closer to Gatwick, another of London's four airports. So, to cover his arse, he'd come up with…

I chartered a helicopter to make the hop from Gatwick to Stansted, and I was headed there when…

She'd see the photo and check it out on a traffic app. A bulletproof excuse. Creative, nice. She'd know he was lying, but she could never prove it if he stuck to his story.

Rob eased the Bentley to a stop by a rickety wooden gate heading into the woods. A nearby sign, bent and twisted in bushes, declared Private Property. He turned into a narrow drive overgrown with greenery, stopping when he saw a flash of white through the trees.

A house?

He stopped and made the rest of the way on foot, huddled against a wall of green.

No, not a house, a gate. It was huge, ten or twelve feet high.

Oh, yes... this is the place.

19

Cass stood in the bathroom doorway and stared at Ted's twisted body sprawled in the bloodstained bed linen. He'd been her jailer, her enemy, a person whose existence had consumed her attention on a 24-hour basis. But now he was just a problem, a mess that had to be cleaned up. Day after day, she'd dreamed and plotted, planning for freedom day and what she'd do with it. Top of her list was *tell the police*. At first, she'd expected them to come bursting through the door at any moment, men in balaclavas huddling behind bulletproof shields, masked avengers lobbing stun grenades and brandishing machine guns. But watching the news with Ted, or more accurately the no-news-about-me news, and seeing that docudrama photo set—*Rob and Priscilla, A Love Story*, she'd accepted the truth. Rob hadn't reported her abduction, and like everything else in her life, she would have to take care of it herself. Despite this setback, one thing had never altered throughout her freedom campaign. When she finally made it, she'd march into the nearest police station and holler and make damn sure every word out of her mouth damaged both Ted and Rob.

But all that was history.

This was the now.

The mess.

A dead man garroted by a choker of his own design and at his own command, although not intentionally and not by accident. Try explaining that to a hardnose detective. Not forgetting the other side of the equation. Zoe had become Cass. But her new name and hairstyle didn't offload her childhood, and the Ivy League idioms she'd put on show when the occasion demanded didn't wash away the stains left by growing up on a street the world had forgotten. No child should have to jam a chair against their bedroom door to stop their father's drunken predations or wonder who that strange man was counting out pills and pouring powders in their mother's bedroom. Now that child was a woman looking at unfettered access to bank accounts stuffed with so much money she had to count the zeros with her fingers. So no, there'd be no police. This recent turn of events had wiped her long-held vision of justice clean off her memory. Justice was a feel-good moment, a string of zeros in her bank account was a feel-good forever.

She went downstairs and drank a glass of wine, sitting at the kitchen table, swallowing it in thirsty-man gulps, her eyes roaming around her—fresh eyes, appraising and valuing. All this was hers now if she wanted it. There might be a way to figure that out. But a better option was the path of least resistance, pillage his bank accounts, take the money and run. The only obstacle was the mess upstairs and that was solvable. Ted would disappear. He was sure to have plenty of gardening equipment, high-tech stuff she could use to dig a deep hole. She'd reconnoiter the garages and storage areas and find something. In the short-term, she could stash him in the freezer. After that, she'd study the finances in more detail and make a plan. That was a moment to look forward to. She'd open some new accounts, then scoot a few million into them and stick a pile into untraceable crypto. Living with Rob and his endless cackling about crypto markets, she'd absorbed a ton of strategies by osmosis. With her financial future secure, she'd shuffle on down to the Med and buy a villa on an island overlooking the sea.

Which one?

She'd visit them all, then decide. She picked up her empty wineglass and stared at it.

Gone already.

Another glass would be nice but she had work to do. She slipped on rubber gloves and went out into the hall. There was a worn Persian rug there that would make a perfect body bag. She carried it upstairs and spread it out on the floor by the bed with Ted's ice-blue marble eyes following her every move. She so wanted to close them. But she couldn't bring herself to touch his skin even with gloves on. Grabbing him by his sock-covered ankles, she dragged him off the bed. He hit the floor with a thump, his body first and his head following up with a crunch that echoed in the stillness. Averting her eyes, she rolled the carpet around him and dragged him out of the bedroom and along the landing to the top of the stairs.

She took a break there. Ted was heavy, and the woven underside of the rug created a lot of friction with the carpeted surface beneath it. She surveyed the route down the stairway. There were two flights of stairs to the ground floor. In between was a stair landing lit by sunlight streaming in from the window. A hairpin bend. That was tricky. The body wasn't stiff yet but the carpet cocoon made bending it problematic, and at all costs, she had to keep his blood off the floor. Cleaning up the bedroom would be work enough. Yes, she had decided to tidy up. This was her home now, albeit temporarily, and that meant a spring clean. She already had an explanation for her presence should anyone call in person. She was Ted's interior designer. He was on a trip, sailing to the Bahamas, and he'd given her the keys to get the place upgraded in his absence.

Why don't you send him an email? He checks his mailbox regularly.

Then she could confirm the story as Ted when they followed up.

Her plan in place, she repositioned herself, standing a few steps down from the body and grabbing his legs.

Heave.

She inched down step-by-step with the body sliding downhill easily in her wake until—

The phone rang.

Ted's phone of course. And not a call or a message. She'd heard both those ringtones already. She snatched it out of her back pocket and took a step down to get her footing, turning away from the body.

INCURSION.

An alert in red letters.

Flash-flash-flash.

She clicked on the link and...

"Oh, my God..."

Her hand went to her mouth, her face blank with shock. Then her fingers curled around her mouth to stifle a giggle.

Rob.

He was skulking behind a bush, looking this way and that. He darted in a half crouch from the bush to a garden shed and disappeared behind it.

My ninja has finally come to rescue me, she thought.

But then the smile faded.

My lover who never contacted the police...

She let that die there, stifling the rage. At least he'd shown up, and in just a few days. But why was he flying solo on a Mission Impossible extraction of his maiden in distress if he was abandoning her for Pix?

Ted's security system lived up to his hype with its CCTV cameras following Rob as he scurried from the shed to a rhododendron bush, having equipped himself enroute with an ax.

Cass looked back at Ted. No way could she leave him there. She slipped the phone into her pocket and lifted his legs, planning to haul him back onto the landing. Once she had him up there, she could drag him back to the bedroom and shut the door. But the moment she hoisted his legs off the step, his body slalomed down the staircase and she had to jump aside to avoid getting taken along for the ride. He ended up on the stair landing, propped up against the wall in a puddle of sunlight, dead eyes looking down into the reception hall. A string of curses hit her lips but was silenced by the sound of breaking glass.

The kitchen… the back door.

He was breaking in.

Of course, he was. He was hardly going to knock at the front door with an ax. But that was a blessing. Standing at the front door, he'd have had a direct line of sight at the stairwell.

Hi Rob, welcome to The Manor. Say hi to Ted. He'll show you to your room.

She checked herself for blood stains, found none, and hurried down to the kitchen.

So this was it. The reunion. The alpha male hero bursts into the evil goblin's lair and snatches the golden-haired princess up in his arms.

Only not.

Rob was at the other end of the kitchen, both hands on the ax handle, the blade raised above his shoulder. Cass froze in the doorway at the other end of the room, the long wooden table between them.

"Where is he?" Rob hissed between clenched teeth, his eyes bobbing around the kitchen like Ted might jump out of the oven and set upon him. None of this was funny. But Cass was having trouble keeping a straight face. If tripping on stress was possible, this was it. The past 24 adrenaline-soaked hours had flipped her from mountainous peaks to bottomless valleys and its afterburn was pure *what the heck*!

"He's gone. I'm free. Don't worry."

"Gone where?" Rob spun his head some more. She'd never seen him like this. He was so pumped it was unreal. She almost wished Ted had been there. What a scene that would have been.

"Out of the picture. Gone. Overseas. Don't worry."

"And left you?" He was lowering the ax, unwinding his ninja crouch, his face wrinkling up, not making sense of this. "You're free?... Then why didn't you leave?"

"I was about to. Calm down. It's all just happened. Put the ax down."

He followed through, lowering it at last, his eyes warily scanning the room. "Sit down." Cass went to the fridge. "Need a beer?" He didn't answer, but he did sit. Cass flipped the top off a beer bottle and passed it to him across the table. He put down the ax and took a long draft of the beer while she poured herself a glass of wine and sat opposite him.

"It's so weird," he said, "finding you like this. I was expecting—"

"Cheers." She raised her glass, an opportune toast to stop his prattling. She let him swig more cold beer, hoping it would cool him off. But as soon as he got his mouth back, he went straight into righteous mode like he was disappointed to have missed out on cleaving Ted's head open with his ax.

"I mean... walking in the kitchen like that. It was like you—"

"What?"

His eyes dropped to the table and he sucked the last of his beer. This was the biggie. Cass knew all his tells. When he looked up towards heaven, he was about to lie, and when he looked down towards hell, he was nervous.

"I'm not saying… but it was like… you were the lady of the house."

"Like I was in it with him, you mean?"

"No, no… that's not it."

Cass stared, stony faced. Not that she had nothing to say. She had plenty. It was to keep that Cape Canaveral blastoff of anger in her chest from making her grab the ax and use it on him. In the end, she hid the explosion behind a sip of wine. This wasn't the moment to go bang. This was the moment to let contempt speak through her eyes. Rob put the bottle down and leaned back in the chair. Or was that shrunk back?

"It's a day for surprises all around," Cass said. "No police. Instead, I get Rob on his lonesome with an ax. I'm surprised you didn't arrive swinging on vines from tree to tree."

"Hey, I just meant…"

"So, where are the police?"

He picked up the empty beer bottle, checked its contents and put it down. She wanted to say, "Get it yourself." But she wanted him to stay put a lot more. She didn't want him wandering around. She'd have to explain Ted's dead body at some point. But he'd go into medical-grade shock at that point, and she needed important issues covered before then. She fetched him another bottle, then skidded the opener across the table to him. At least he could do some work.

"He said he'd kill you. After you got that call through to me and said a few words, it went quiet. Then he came on the line and said if I called the police, he'd kill you."

"And you believed him?"

He popped out a theatrical snort with a shrug of his big chest. "You mean... and take the chance? So how am I supposed to feel when they find bits of you in a ditch?" Me, me, me, she thought. I'd be chopped up in mud and he'd feel bad. Boo-hoo. "I found you, didn't I? I've gone through bloody hell." He poked a finger at her, bristling indignance. "I expected to find you in chains and here you are—"

"Thank God Priscilla was there to hold your hand, or whatever it was needed holding."

"I wouldn't have found you without her."

"I'm so grateful. Remind me to give her a hug next time I catch her in your bed."

"Seriously? That's what you think. Grow up. You've never liked her."

"So you're not having an affair?"

He jumped up, chair legs grating and skipping on stone tiles, then snatched up the beer, and for a split second, she was ready to duck. But no. He was as guilty as sin and that would have taken a righteous man. He drained it, squeezing out silent snarls between gulps. Then he banged the empty bottle down on the table. "We're going. Getting out of here. I've had enough of this nonsense. He told me he'd kill you. That's the truth. And that's the end of that conversation. Now let's go."

Cass didn't budge.

Kill me?

She was still wondering about that. It didn't sound like Ted. Way too ballsy. But if it was a lie, it was a damn good one. Luckily, she had another line of inquiry to fall back on.

"The day I was taken, I spoke to Priscilla. She told me about the detective. I thought maybe you were uncomfortable contacting the police?"

"Oh, that?" There it was, eyes rolling up to heaven and back. "It turned out to be nothing. Some issue in the States. It was all ironed out."

"Okay. So nothing to do with the fraudulent cash you were stuffing into the Antigua bank account with my name on the power of attorney. That's good news."

Rob stared at her, his mouth easing open half an inch, but nothing coming out of it. Cass paid him no mind, a new plan mapping itself out live in her head. She stood up and pulled the phone from her back pocket as if prompted by a vibration.

She checked the screen, then bade Rob sit with a wave of her fingers, a worried look clouding her eyes. She dropped the phone to her side and whispered, "Cops," mouthing the word big in case the sound didn't reach him. "The front gate." She stuck the phone to her ear. "Hello." She waited, shuffling around, acting out nervous agitation. "Mr. Sharpe isn't here. He's overseas. ... I'm his interior designer. He gave me the keys. I'm refurbishing the place. What's this all about? ... No, I've never seen that man before." She spun back to Rob, mouthed *photo* and stabbed an index finger at him. "Yes, of course, leave your card in the mailbox. I'll call you if I see him." A few more pauses and platitudes and it was done, the call over. She pulled the phone away from her ear and stared at it. "They didn't believe me. I'm sure of it."

Rob got up and reached for the phone. "Give me."

"They said they're looking for you. They have a warrant?" She put the phone in her back pocket.

"Look, about that bank account." His eyes found the floor and when they found their way back to her, he said, "I'd been meaning to tell you for—"

"Later. There's no time for that now. I've got an idea. Follow me." She strode out of the kitchen and took a sharp turn under the stairs to the basement door. It was a risk taking him through the hall, but as long as he didn't veer off track, he'd never get sight of Ted. She led him down the ramp. The wine rack was still pulled back and the door to the apartment was open. "They'll never find you here, even if they search the place."

Rob followed her, bewilderment shriveling his face with wrinkles.

"How would they know I'm here? I don't get it—"

"Dammit, I'm trying to help you. Lord knows why. Did they track your phone?" Rob pulled his phone out of his pocket and looked at it forlornly. "For goodness sake, turn it off. Here..." She snatched it out of his hand and turned it off. He took it back, another puzzle riddling his brow.

"How come you've got a phone app linked to the entry system?" Rob's brain was running about three minutes behind events, but this was a warning signal. He was catching up fast. "Is that his phone?"

"You can rest here in the lounge." Cass had to keep this moving. "It's quite comfortable, and there's a kitchenette in back. You'll find drinks and snacks there. Like this—if they come back with a search warrant—we're covered." She left him in the middle of the living room, a puzzled look on his face, and was heading towards the door when she spun back as if struck with a thought. His mouth was already open, another awkward question framing on his lips, but she got there first. "Do you think we'll ever get over this and get back to how we once were?" Her voice was light and upbeat like she was rehearsing for a remake of *The Sound of Music*. As expected, her sudden change of mood hit him like a cruise missile.

"Oh, Cass... yes." He took a step towards her, his arms opening, primed for the embrace. He was so damn guilty even a tiny thread of hope thrown his way looked like a lifeline, something to haul himself back into her good graces.

"Later." She held up both hands to ward him off, and with that, she was gone, locking the door behind her. She leaned with her back against it, a lopsided smile curling her lips. Oh boy... that felt good. She went to Ted's control room—her control room—and checked the apartment's CCTV. Rob was still standing where she'd left him. He was turning around and around, that befuddled look she'd seen earlier returning and darkening the euphoria of her upbeat farewell. She left him to it, running up the ramp to the hall. So much to do and so little time.

Rob sat on the edge of the couch, elbows on knees, his chin resting on the knuckles of his clenched fists—his thinker with a problem pose. He'd been like that a long time, nibbling at his knuckles now and again in deep reflection. Two interlinked events troubled him, the unexpected arrival of the police and the mysterious reincarnation of Cass as the mistress of the house, this house, not his house. The questions that spun off these quantum shocks were hitting him so fast he couldn't answer a single one. The cop on his tail was the most pressing concern. The issues relating to Cass, he could sort out at leisure. But the cops already! That needed an explanation. Cass had suggested his phone. Surely it hadn't got to that level yet.

Pix?

He checked his watch. The jet would be warming up, engines whistling. She'd be on it, waiting. He pulled out his phone and turned it on. To hell with the police. Cass was right. They'd never find him here, even if they searched the place. Sharpe's jail was a hidden fortress. He could see that already. So how had she gotten out of it? And where was he? Rob filed these questions with all the others and turned his attention back to the phone. Stuck in traffic on the M25, he'd set it on Do Not Disturb when her text messages had turned nasty. He steeled himself and checked through the messages and voicemails. There were double digits of both.

The most recent voice message was lengthy.

Oh, dear...

It was detailed and incorporated an impressive range of expletives, some in unique and imaginative ways. She threatened to call the cops if he didn't show up RIGHT NOW, but she didn't admit to doing it. All that was academic anyway. He was buried in a basement fortress in darkest Sussex with cops lurking in the forest beyond. He'd burned the Pix bridge. But at least he'd found Cass and she was okay. More or less okay. Something weird was going on. That was for sure.

He stood up and wandered around the apartment, checking it out distractedly, one eye still on his thoughts. He'd never been much of a look back in anger guy. The future was always where his mind settled best. The future was like wet clay, malleable, ready to create anything you could imagine, whereas the past was cast in stone and most of his best forgotten. Pix was history, the Pix/Cass conundrum no longer a wall he had to sit uncomfortably astride. His future was with Cass and the number one priority was getting her out of this house and then out of the country. If they were on a jet right now heading to the Caribbean, all these troubling issues would get burned to a crisp in their vapor trail. He flitted off momentarily, enjoying the flight in his head until his thoughts crashed into rock-hard reality—the British Virgin Islands, Blockchain Analytics, and its Antigua bank account.

The money pump.

How had she found out about all that? Had she been going through his papers?

No way.

He wasn't dumb enough to leave a physical paper trail.

Fielding Cass as his proxy had seemed like such a smart move. But now, it looked more like a bomb going tick-tock. No point in speculating how she came about the information, he had to deal with it, and that meant sucking up to her big time. The Cass-Rob relationship axis had to be stabilized. From here on out, he had to be helpful and loving, and above all, avoid confrontation.

"Rob…" He spun around. He hadn't heard her come in, and it sounded like she was right behind him. But no. He looked up at the wall screen as her face filled it. "I took a walk to peek out into the lane there. The gate cameras don't reach that far. Anyway, the cops are still there… just one car, about 50 yards up the road. There were two uniforms in it and they were talking on the radio."

"They probably—"

"I'm going to make us some dinner. We can spend the night in the apartment and eat dinner down there. It'll be best. I'll check again in the morning."

"I think we should—"

"I'll be about an hour. Why don't you get some rest?"

And with that, the screen went blank.

"Cass." He waited, his hands on his hips. "Cass, I need to talk to you. … Now."

Nothing. No reply. Just a blank screen.

Rob muttered irritably and walked off, his casual look around turning edgy, now more like an inspection.

Amazing bedroom.

He checked the mattress, prodding it with stiff fingers.

Firm, nice.

That stopped him in his tracks.

Did Sharpe? Did they…?

He gave the bed a second look. He'd have to get that out of her later. That was part and parcel of this whole question. How did she get to be the lady of the house? And where the hell was Sharpe?

He checked the dressing room next, his concern ratcheting up as he flipped through the racks of clothes.

Her size, her style, and...

He jerked out a printed floral dress and checked the label.

DoubleJ?

He'd seen that dress. She'd showed it to him on a web store. She'd asked him if he thought it was too feminine for her. He couldn't remember his answer—whatever had come into his head most likely—but here it was in Sharpe's basement. He rifled through the racks and drawers with Pix's accusation ringing louder and louder in his head.

Maybe she's in it with him. Maybe he's her boyfriend.

He pulled himself up sharply when he caught sight of his face in the mirror. Anger. It was pulsing there like a beacon. He had to pull himself together, get back on plan. *Be helpful, loving, convivial and above all, avoid confrontation.* In his harried state, that was going to be a struggle. He breathed in through the nose and out through his mouth, four or five big breaths, filling himself with air from his belly to his throat, an old rugby trick that had stopped him punching guys out more than once. He went to the bathroom and washed his face and hands. When he came out, he heard Cass moving around in the living area. He took another one of those long cooling breaths, muttered his mantra—*helpful, loving, convivial*—stretched a smile across his lips and joined her.

His agenda clear, Rob was voluble as they munched through salad and sipped red wine, assiduously avoiding everything he wanted to ask her. They were all booby-trapped with confrontation. He'd get to them, but only when the opportunity arose, when Cass veered close to an opening he could slip through without sparking a conflagration. With all that in mind, he stuck to the future, their future, his mythical vision of their new life together in the paradise awaiting them.

So far, so good…

But eating the steaks, the mood shifted. Cass was not getting the future paradise vibe. She kept using phrases like problematic issues, resolving differences and healing wounds. In fact, they were showing up in every sentence. So by the time they pushed their plates aside, it was clear to him that he'd have to endure a little pain to earn the dream future he was touting. He'd have to pay the piper for past misdeeds.

"For example," Cass said, staring at him but not finishing her sentence. Rob waited, but then wilted, giving her what she wanted, his full attention eye to eye. "No more lying. A spring clean, starting now. All those shitty lies stinking up our closet, they all get tossed in the truth dumpster. Agreed?"

Rob winced like he'd had his balls pinched with sharp fingernails.

"Of course. It's the only way."

"Priscilla?"

"You're right, or half right at least. She's always had a crush on me. She came on to me a couple of times. I wanted to fire her. But she threatened to file a wrongful dismissal sexual harassment suit against me, accusing me of sacking her because she'd refused me. It was all bullshit, of course."

"So her obsession came to nothing?"

"Only in her imagination."

Cass nodded and slid her empty wineglass towards him. He dutifully filled it—they were on their second bottle—while she picked up her phone and whipped her finger back and forth across its screen. Rob waited.

She'd turned quiet. Never a good sign. He pushed her wineglass invitingly towards her, but she ignored it and looked up at the wall TV. Rob's eyes swiveled up to it as it burst into life and he froze.

A booth in a restaurant, a lush one, Pix, her head resting back on the seat, her long neck twisted and white, Rob's face buried in hers, the fingertips of his big right hand stroking her swan-like neck, its palm hovering over breasts bulging out of a tight black bodice.

"She's got some imagination," Cass said. "Looks like reality to me." She swiped her finger once more. "This is one of my favorites. Not the most saucy, by a long way." Rob kept his eyes on the screen as he put down his glass with an unsteady hand.

A park bench.

He remembered the day. They'd spent a couple of hours in a hotel and stopped on their way back to the office for some heavy chat about 'us.' It had gotten emotional and they'd ended up virtually making out on the bench. "What was your hand doing in this one? Straightening out her—what would she call them?—knickers. Oh yes, straightening out her knickers for her. What a gentleman."

"Okay, okay."

"You lied. Not the best of starts to our coupledom spring clean, is it?"

"I'm trying to avoid confrontation. That's why I lied. The important thing is it's over. I dumped her today. I told her it was over. I'd found you, and she'd have no part in my future. She was furious. Those police that showed up at the door, how did they know I was here? They weren't following me. She threatened to call the police, and obviously, that's what she did. All she had to do was give them the name. Edward Sharpe. The police would find the house in an instant. It took me hours. I was a right bloody Columbo by the way."

"Police. Yes. And the financial thing, as you call it. So tell me about that."

"There was never any intent to defraud. I authorized a series of legitimate payments—"

"To a research company that apparently I run."

"I can explain that."

"I don't doubt it. But to a dummy like me, it looks like you set up a shell company linked to me to funnel money to companies controlled by you. And if that didn't look fishy enough, where is the research you paid a billion dollars for?"

"It's research, risk money, sometimes it doesn't yield..."

Rob's eyes took over from his mouth, zooming up to the TV screen as more images rolled on by with Cass picking up the narrative.

"Account Opening Form blah blah, Power of Attorney blah blah. Cassandra Beauvoir. Look! I'm all over the place. I had no idea I was so important, and it must be me because that's my signature, or else it's a first-class forgery. Now what would the police say if—"

"I was going to tell you. But the right moment never—"

"Right moment? To tell me you'd implicated me in a financial crime that could cost me years in jail. You'd have to wait a long time for that moment."

"I was in a tight spot. I needed a—"

"Mug. Isn't that the British word? Some dumb asshole you could put one over on."

"It was only temporary. I planned to bankrupt the company before the shit hit the fan. Crypto firms go tits up all the time, especially dodgy offshore outfits. I needed a strawman. And I knew I could trust you."

"Sure you could. You can always trust someone who doesn't know fuck about what's happening. I was the perfect patsy, someone you weren't related to and, as you kept postponing our wedding, someone whose status as a third party was guaranteed to stay the same."

Cass went back to her phone, swiping through page after page, her slideshow drip-feeding resignation on his downcast face.

How on earth had she...?

Of course... he spun his head back to Cass. That wasn't her phone. He'd found her phone on the floor in the summerhouse.

"Edward Sharpe," he said, like a judge announcing a defendant. The bastard. It was him. He'd fixed the hacking problem. He'd needed super administrator credentials to do that. So the IT department had trusted him with the keys to the firm's digital safe. He'd had access to everything, the data on every computer, all the applications and security protocols. He'd spent days cracking the ransomware locks. But evidently, some of that time had been spent spying and uploading malware. He'd gotten into Rob's laptop and from there, he'd hopped into his phone. He'd taken the photos too. He'd stalked them both and he'd told Cass everything. From the moment he'd walked through the kitchen door, she'd been playing cat and mouse with him. She knew everything, not only about his cheating, but his entire offshore setup. A hot flash of anger roared in his chest, but it soon burned out. She'd humiliated him with cold calculation. She'd put him to the test and he'd failed miserably. He'd already lost Pix today. Now he'd lost Cass. He looked at her with sad dog eyes.

She met his gaze, studying it, thinking about something.

But what?

She stood up. "I guess that's enough for today. Would you like a cup of tea? I've got Earl Grey. We can take one last shot at straightening this out in the morning." A bone! She'd tossed him a bone. "We'd better stay down here in case they come back with a search warrant."

"You're not going to call the police on me, are you?"

She shook her head. "I'm a bitch, not a snitch."

Rob nodded, no problem with that. A bitch he could live with.

Cass left him to sip his Earl Grey tea and went to sit in a hot bath. That was all for the best. He needed time alone, time to think. Driving down from London, all he could think of was finding her safe, rescuing her and being with her. Now all that had been turned on its head. She'd locked him in stocks and pounded him with feces. She knew every misstep he'd ever taken, every misdeed he'd ever chanced. Sure, he'd cheated and played fast and loose with a few legal niceties, and yes, he'd been less than forthright concerning her role in his master plan. But she didn't see those as misdemeanors. To her, they were felonies. So realistically, how were they ever going to recover? The more he shuffled the day's events back and forth through his get-real machine, the more the obvious emerged.

Rob and Cass were history, their *us* days done and dusted.

She'd never respect him after this. Worse, she had him under her thumb. And this *take one last shot at this in the morning* crap could be just that. Bullshit. She could call the cops anytime. The tinkle of alarm bells was soon a deafening belfry boom. Even if he walked out on her, he wouldn't be safe. She had this paperwork. That and her testimony spelled doom in a court of law. *Damn*. This had gone so wrong. He'd have been better off on that jet with Pix.

Tension got him up on his feet and he paced, but one foot caught on the other and he stumbled, catching the fall with his hand on the back of the couch.

How much did I drink?

A few bottles of wine, a few beers, not enough to....

Must be the stress. What a fucking day!

He went to the bedroom and lay on the bed. Cass was singing in the bath, her voice filtering out as a melody, one of those sad old French songs she loved. Must be the Beauvoir genes. *No regrets*, something like that. The moment kindled a warm memory, but he dampened that to nothing and got his woozy mind back on the issue at hand.

I'm in a shit hole.

That much was blindingly obvious. But the more he thought about it, the more he realized there was an emergency exit. Cass had disappeared. No, he hadn't reported it, but he had excuses for that. He also had plenty of witnesses to prove he'd played no part in her disappearance. Quite the opposite, he'd made huge efforts to find her and succeeded.

But what if I found her dead?

Murdered by that bastard Sharpe. He'd stalked her, abducted her and murdered her. He'd also framed Rob by conducting illicit financial transactions. Yes, all he needed was an ace lawyer, one of those fifty-thousand-a-day KCs. He'd even get Pix back. With Cass out of the picture, that'd be the easiest part of it. Pix was flexible. Shower her with money and gifts and she'd be crawling around at his feet cooing love songs.

No regrets?

Thanks Cass. Good idea.

But could he do it? Did he have the stomach for it?

When you've got no choice, doesn't everyone?

21

Cass leaned back in her leather chair and stretched her legs under the desk. The chair was ridiculously comfortable, one of those gaming chairs for rich nerds who spent eighteen hours at a stretch playing *Call of Duty*. She was about to eat breakfast, her appetite sharpened by the aroma of hot coffee and freshly baked croissants, unmissable in the confines of the control room. Her eyes were on the wall screens with every room in the apartment covered, except for the bathroom and dressing room, of course.

Good old truthful Ted, the exception that proved the rule. Some men didn't lie. Too bad he was... well, Ted and not Rob.

Dinner had been a test, one last chance for Rob to come clean, and he hadn't just failed. He'd crashed and burned. He'd looked her in the eye, put his hand on his heart and lied. So she'd humiliated him, heaping it on.

Too late now to second-guess how wise that was.

Trust, respect, admiration, all the qualities that build the foundation of love, they'd all gone up in flames. Rob was smart, weaselly, but smart. So what would he make of all this? As she watched his inert body sleeping off her Mickey, she knew she'd done the right thing. She'd taken control and made the call. His pride would never let him forgive her, and at a practical level, she knew where he'd buried the skeletons. She'd always have that on him. There was no going back to what they were, and the trail of what they might have been was a mirage best left to fade.

Her eyes zoomed in on his movement. He rolled one way, then back, reaching out vaguely, still out of it. He'd slept on top of the covers with his clothes on, shirt buttons undone, belt loose and his shoes kicked off. She'd overdone the Valium. She'd put a starter dose—two 10 mg tablets—in his salad dressing, while hers had been eaten plain. He'd washed those down with copious glasses of wine, and after he'd flunked his truth test, she'd served up her special cocktail, Earl Grey tea with a fistful of crushed pills. Big man that he was, he'd lasted an hour or two after supping that before passing out. Now here he was resurfacing sixteen hours later with a comfort break well overdue. He rolled about some more, then sat on the edge of the bed and looked around, black rings circling his eyes, his face grumpy and sallow, his big muscles hanging like sacks. A grizzly bear rousing itself after a cold winter was the picture that came to mind, although she'd never seen a grizzly, and after this, she wouldn't need to. He got to his feet and wobbled, sticking out a paw and waving it to catch his balance. He was disoriented, and it took him a minute or two to find the bathroom. With no cameras there, she had to imagine this part, but writing the script wasn't hard. The bathroom was full of mirrors. It wouldn't take him long to notice...

The toilet flushed.

Wait for it!

The bathroom door burst open, slamming against the wall as he stormed back into the bedroom.

"Cass, where the fuck are you?"

He stood by the bed, his hands on the choker, spinning it around and looking for the latch with his fingers.

Good luck with that, pal.

He soon gave up and marched through the living room to the exit door.

Oops... no handle.

He'd been too preoccupied the night before to have noticed it. He bunched his fists and beat the door like a drum. That apartment was soundproof, but he was whacking it so hard she heard it even in the control room.

Enough fun and games.

She lit up the TV in the living room.

"You're awake at last. I was getting worried. You must have been exhausted and—"

"What's this?" He yanked on the choker. "What are you playing at?"

"That? Don't worry about that. I'll be down directly and explain everything. What you need is a strong cup of coffee and I've got some freshly baked croissants here. Freshly microwaved anyways."

He backed away from the door, but his fists were still curled. She picked up the tray, took it out into the basement and unlocked the apartment door.

"Here you are," she said, hurrying past him into the dining room and setting up breakfast on the table. He followed, his frown darker with each step. She poured a cup of coffee, added milk and sugar and offered it to him.

He ignored it, thrusting his head up close to her face, his neck muscles flexing with sinew like an Olympic weightlifter going for gold.

"What the fuck is this?"

Ding-a-ling.

The F word again.

When they'd met, Rob had sprinkled every other sentence with it, but she'd trained him out of it. Zoe didn't give a fuck about swearing, but she'd never heard Cass use any kind of profanity. So she'd adopted the same high standards, admonishing his trash talk every time it came out of his mouth. Keen to hide his humble roots, Rob had complied, restricting its use to moments immediately prior to a loud bang.

"Calm down, please. I'll explain everything. Have some coffee and sit down."

He made a show of regaining control, his post fuck-word regimen, a long deep breath, his chest and six-pack on full show. "I am calm. Coffee after. Explanation now. Why am I wearing this"—he put his fingers up to the choker and fiddled with it—"poof's jewelry."

Cass poured herself a cup of coffee. This had to be dealt with and it was never going to be a moment of calm. That said, his beer-wine-Valium hangover was putting a dangerous edge on his anger.

"It may look like jewelry and that's how it started its life. But it's been..." She stopped. Why bother to sweet talk? There was no way to soft-soap this. "It's a restraint. Voice activated. I switched it from Ted's voice to mine. This was the one I wore. It used to be called Cassbot. But I renamed it Rob-bot, or Robot for short. Watch. Robot activate." Rob looked down, a reflex to the momentary vibration. "There's a tiny LED that flashes on, then turns off. That's it."

"Restraint?"

"You're going to have to take my word for that. Ted showed me a video, but I haven't had time to make one for you. So I'll leave that to your imagination. Let's just say it's not called a choker for nothing."

"Take it off." He stepped towards her and turned around so she could reach the clasp at the back.

"I can't do that now. Maybe later. When we've sorted everything out."

He turned to face her, his eyes narrow and twisted. She'd never seen him like that. Scary. She sipped her coffee, both hands on the cup to keep them steady.

"Everything? As in?"

"You and me. Our futures."

"Futures?"

My, my… dopey he might be, but he'd picked up on the plural.

"Yours and mine. There's all these loose ends to tie up, and dirty secrets we need to—"

He slapped the cup out of her hands and it bounced on the table, slewing a wave of hot coffee on the breakfast tray. She'd barely opened her mouth to gasp when he had her by the throat, spinning her around and bending her back over the table. He jerked her twice, banging her head on the solid wood surface, the hot coffee burning her back.

"I'll show you choker. You take this off or I'll—"

"Robot choke." Her voice barely made it past his steel grip, and what did get past was so squeaky she wondered if it would work. But then she saw it—the double flash of the choker's LED followed by the whine of its tiny but oh-so-strong motor. Rob didn't flinch, still holding her by the throat, his thumbs pressing into vital pipelines, pain squeezing her eyes to the edge of their sockets. Her head spun, no way to speak now, his face dissolving as if sinking in clouded water. Then suddenly she was free, sucking down raucous gasps of air. Rob was stumbling back, grabbing his throat. His gym-tight neck muscles had shrugged off the choker's first efforts, but Ted's first-class engineering had won the battle in the end. She dragged herself upright, leaning back on the table and massaging her throat. Rob swayed, taking tiny steps back and forth like a drunk man trying to avoid the inevitable, his arms waving on either side looking for balance or something to grab onto. His eyes caught Cass and he lunged at her but never made it, crashing on his knees and falling forward on all fours. She waited, hoping she'd gotten the recalibration right, the last thing she needed was another dead body.

Finally... *thump*.

He keeled over and hit the floor.

"Robot release."

The choker loosened. She kneeled beside him and checked the pulse in his throat. It was pounding. He was unconscious but he'd live. Her collar size guesstimate had been spot on. Luckily, she'd bought him a few shirts over the years. He'd be out for a while after a choking like that. So she headed for the bathroom and cleaned up, then changed her coffee stained clothes. Rob was halfway to his feet when she came back into the living room, pumping air in and out of his oxygen starved body. She stopped a couple of yards away from him.

"Now you've had the demo. I'm sure you won't need a sequel." He swiveled his head to look up at her, his downcast expression reassuring. The Robot had choked all the fight out of him. She took a few steps closer, pulled up a chair and sat on it. "Rest a moment. Then we'll take a walk in the garden and you can get some fresh air." He glanced up at her again, then slumped on his backside, her proposal accepted. "Remember our first date? You were the cofounder of CoinAxis, the world's fastest-growing crypto exchange, and I was the duly impressed newbie at your agency's art department. So before we got to the bedroom chitchat part of our conversation, you told me all about risk/benefit and how you needed big balls to play the game. I can't help thinking there was a bit of advertising going on at that point. But anyway, I listened as you—"

"The coin toss," he said. "I asked if you'd toss a coin with the—"

"Future of humanity at stake. If it came down heads, there'd be no more war, poverty, disease or climate change."

"But if it came down tails, a nuclear holocaust would wipe us all out. And I offered you the coin of fate."

"And I wouldn't take it. So you tossed it and wiped out humanity."

"That's supposed to explain why you fitted me with the psycho's collar?"

"It explains the difference between us. No way do I make a fifty-fifty call when oblivion is one of the prizes. We're never going to make it after this, whatever I choose to forget. Your pride won't permit it. Sooner or later, you'll realize—if you haven't already—my testimony can put you in jail. If we were an item, it wouldn't matter. But those days are over. So there I'd be, an aggrieved ex, floating out there somewhere with a library of *send Rob to jail* docs. Why take the risk when there's a simple solution? I've already been disappeared—conveniently by another man—why not keep it that way?"

"You think I'd kill you?"

"You're the risk/benefit guru. I see zero downside and a rosy dawn upside. Sharpe takes the blame for disappearing Cass, and you get the perfect fall guy, a vanished ex you can blame anything you want on."

"I still don't get it... why this?" He yanked on the Robot.

"I'm heading overseas. But before I go, there are a few fun facts about the choker I need to teach you, like what happens if you try to leave the property. Long story short, you end up dead. So make yourself comfortable. I'll be taking your phone, but there's plenty for you to do. Nice gym and swimming pool. When I'm comfortable and safe, and far away, I'll FedEx a package with a password that will get you into the computer in the control room, along with instructions for removing the choker." He went to speak, his face screwing with objections, but Cass wasn't having any of it. She stood up and offered him her hand. "Let's take that walk." He looked at her hand, some argument still festering inside him, but then took it and struggled up on his feet.

Cass led him out of the apartment, up the ramp and through the kitchen to the utility room where she stood by the freezer.

"Take a good look at this." She lifted the lid. Rob yelped and recoiled, banging against a stack of shelves behind him. Cass took in his reaction, then followed his manic gaze down into the freezer. "Rob, meet Edward Sharpe. Ted, this is Rob. You've already spoken over the phone, I believe." Cass hadn't had time to remove the food, so she'd dumped Ted on top of it. His head was resting on a pillow of microwave ready gourmet dinners and his eyes stared up at them, his throat arched, the bright blue and pastel shades of the choker showcased in a deep purple frame of congealed blood. His butt and back were nestled in a hollow, his knees bent, his legs scrunched up over his body like a yoga posture of moderate difficulty. "Tell me. What do you see?"

Rob didn't answer at first, his head spinning back and forth between her and the freezer. The color was back in his face already. His heart had to be pounding. "What I see"—his stare broke free from the frozen body and met hers—"is a psychopathic, murdering bitch."

That was harsh. Sharpe had abducted her and treated her like an insect specimen. But it wasn't a bait she was tempted to chew on.

"Mmm... interesting. What I see is no more room in the freezer. I mean... this is one full freezer. I'd never fit another body in here, especially not a big one like yours." She paused long enough for the message to be clear, then leaned in closer. "Hi, my name is Zoe, and if you ever lay a finger on me again without my explicit permission." She pointed down at the freezer. "Just so you know." She turned away from his blank face and took hold of a shovel that was leaning against the wall.

"Zoe?"

"That's all you're getting." She held out the shovel, but he didn't take it. "In case you forget my good advice, we're going to make some room for you. There's a patch of valerian on that south-facing slope behind the house. Painted Ladies feed on its flowers in the late summer. That's a type of butterfly. They migrate from the Mediterranean and they started arriving last week. They were one of Ted's favorites. He got so excited about it. He'd be thrilled to know his body was feeding the flowers that fed them. That would pass for romance in his world."

"You killed him. Now you expect me to bury the body?"

"This was a suicide, not a murder." Cass stared down at the mess of a man scrunched up on a bed of ready-made meals. "I owe him a lot. We both do."

"Owe him?

"He gave me x-ray vision to see right through to the weasel heart"—she stabbed Rob's chest with her finger—"of the man I wanted to marry." Her eyes drifted back to Ted. "He left me a fortune too and helped me find out who I really am."

"What are you talking about?"

"And thanks to Ted, I pulled off the perfect murder."

Rob pointed at the body in the freezer. "You call that perfect?"

"Not him. That was assisted suicide. All I did was facilitate it."

"Then who? And who's Zoe?"

"You don't need the details. Cassandra Beauvoir has vanished, never to be seen again. Maybe she was abducted and her body left in a shallow grave on a windswept moor. Maybe she fled the country to escape prosecution after getting mixed up in a billion-dollar fraud. Who knows? I guarantee no one will ever find her. Cass arrived in the UK, shacked up with you, and then... *poof.* And that's a happy ever after ending for you. Now she'll never be able to contradict your version of events. You might even make out like the bandit you are. Thanks to Ted, you end up with the perfect fall guy, your dead ex."

She grabbed his hand and stuck the shovel in it, giving him a look he didn't need twice. "So you get to dig his grave, by way of thanks." She closed the freezer and opened the door to the garden. "Let's go." Rob followed her into the midday sun, trailing the shovel in his wake. "I can show you the grounds after. It's a beautiful spot."

They walked across the lawn in silence to an unkempt field that swept up towards trees where a red blaze of valerian basked in the sun. Cass sat in the grass nearby and Rob dug, stopping from time to time to sweep the sweat from his brow with his forearm. The butterflies scattered at first, but soon returned. Cass studied the scene with an artist's eye, the toiling man in a field of blooms surrounded by a swarm of Painted Ladies feeding at will.

Nice.
That'd make a nice landscape.
Maybe she'd paint it one day.

22

<u>One year later</u>

Dear Josh,
it's been a long time.

Zoe stopped and reread the line, then put down the pen and looked up. So long, too long. The last time she'd put pen to paper and written Dear Josh, she'd been in India, wiping up tears of failure after she'd tried and failed to get into Afghanistan. The next day she'd headed to Thailand with her new friend Cass. The letters to her brother had started years earlier on the day she'd watched his box carried on the shoulders of six Marines from a plane to a limousine. They'd become part of her life, diary notes shared with a brother loved and lost, heartfelt sentiments, precision cut in her calligraphic handwriting. They'd stopped in Thailand, what had happened on the ferry too much even for her loving brother to forgive. So this moment felt good, reviving the ritual. She didn't need a priest. She had Josh.

She picked up the pen and leaned over the scented paper.

Signing it all off in England worked out as planned. But it took longer than I expected to sort through the logistics of my inheritance. Basically, how to get the money out of where it was and into where I wanted it.

And Rob?

All sorted, as the Brits say. That situation turned out to be easier and quicker than I'd dared to hope.

Lesson learned?

When dealing with a weasel, cut a weasel-sized hole in a nearby fence. They're sure to take it. Last I heard, Mr. and Mrs. Weasel were in Latin America and Rob was advising a wobbly dictatorship on how to supercharge their national economy with his crypto rocket fuel. I can't complain. He buried that sad little man for me, removing the choker from around his neck in case he got dug up one day and someone said, what the...? He also nuked Ted's servers, wiping them clean—photos, videos, audio recordings, endless files. Zap, all gone now. So none of it ever happened.

She looked up, her eyes skimming the infinity pool and peering through a break in the olive greenery at a snatch of blue wedged between craggy white rocks. It was her private cove, a 50-yard walk down a twisty path. She'd head down there later. She did every day at sunset. But this, stopping to stare, she did that a thousand times a day.

She got back to her letter. She had to tell Josh about it, her house. She owned property, dammit, she, Zoe Lynch, the girl most likely never to...

That island to island trek I planned, checking out every chunk of rock in the Mediterranean, well... it never happened. I started off in Mallorca, and that was good enough for me. I found a town called Deia or Deya. Every town in this place has two names, one Catalan, one Spanish. Anyway, this one was made to measure for your sister. It's surrounded by mountains, an artist colony, sort of, loads of writers, musicians, and creative people. A guy called Robert Graves kicked all that off, a British writer. He got his head messed up fighting in the first world war, shell shock, they called it back then. And now there's me, an American artist. I got my head messed up growing up in West Virginia, shit shock, I call that. He healed up nicely here and I'm planning on doing the same thing.

A noise caught her attention. She went to the railing at the edge of the terrace and looked down at the pool. It was Ramon, her pool man, boy more like. He was hardly out of his teens. He waved and gave her a thumbs up, holding the door open with his tight buns as he manhandled the tools of his trade. Zoe went back to her letter, but she'd lost the thread of it.

That's all for now. I'll let you know how it goes.
Love, Sis.

She read the letter twice, virtual sponges in her head and heart sucking all the good out of the feeling it gave her.

A ceramic bowl with a turquoise abstract design sat on the table next to her writing pad and served as an ashtray. She'd bought it in the village after watching the potter craft it. She held the letter above it, picked up a butane barbecue lighter and waved its snaking flame back and forth under it. When it caught, she held it at one corner, angling it this way and that so it would burn slowly and she could follow the spiral of smoke as it drifted skyward.

The ritual complete, she stowed the lighter in the matching ceramic vase next to the bowl.

The choker.

Her hand brushed against it at the bottom of the vase. She'd forgotten it was there. She'd been holding it the day before when her housemaid had shown up early, and she'd dropped it out of sight to avoid any awkward questions. She didn't want Pilar getting curious, or worse yet, finding it and checking it out. This was the Melbot. She took it out and looked at it. Rob had cleaned it up nicely for her. He'd ended up with the Robot, of course, although he might well have renamed it Pixbot by now.

So what will I do with it?

"Señora… Señora Zoe…" She went to the railing and looked down at Ramon, sliding her hand behind her so he wouldn't see the choker. "Next week… Thursday is okay?"

"Sure. What's happening on Wednesday? Big date?"

He chuckled. "No, nothing… I have no… just birthday. I have twenty-one years."

"Wow… congratulations. Big day. I'll get you something."

"No, no…" His face turned serious and he waved his index finger, dismissing the idea. "Thank you, Señora." He waved at the pool. "I finish now."

"See you next Thursday."

He nodded and she watched him finishing his work, leaning against the railing, fingering the choker distractedly.

So what can I get him?

Something easy.

A shirt, maybe.

I wonder what his collar size is.